A Candlelight Ecstasy Romance®

"I'M LEAVING, KATE. ONCE THE POKER GAME IS OVER, I'LL BE GONE."

"That's it?" she asked in pained disbelief. "You're just going to go as if nothing ever happened between us?"

"How can I stay in Still Waters? What would I do here?" he demanded. "I'm a gambler. I make my living off of people like you. My friends are as close to riffraff as you can get and still be out of jail."

"I don't care about that!" she cried angrily. "You can go on playing poker until the cows come home. You can fleece every farmer in Nevada just so long as I can be with you."

"It wouldn't work, honey. Someday you'll see that it just isn't worth it."

"I'm sorry it isn't worth it to you," she said in a choked voice. "Because it would have been worth it to me. But then I fell in love with you. How unbelievably stupid of me."

CANDLELIGHT ECSTASY ROMANCES®

THE GAMBLER'S GAME

Lee Magner

A CANDLELIGHT ECSTASY ROMANCE®

Published by
Dell Publishing Co., Inc.
1 Dag Hammarskjold Plaza
New York, New York 10017

ISBN: 0-440-12794-7

Printed in the United States of America

First printing—January 1986

To Our Readers:

We have been delighted with your enthusiastic response to Candlelight Ecstasy Romances® and we thank you for the interest you have shown in this exciting series.

In the upcoming months, we will continue to present the distinctive sensuous love stories you have come to expect only from Ecstasy. We look forward to bringing you many more books from your favorite authors and also, the very finest work from new authors of contemporary romantic fiction.

As always, we are striving to present the unique, absorbing love stories that you enjoy most—books that are more than ordinary romance. Your suggestions and comments are always welcome. Please write to us at the address below.

Sincerely,

The Editors
Candlelight Romances
1 Dag Hammarskjold Plaza
New York, New York 10017

CHAPTER ONE

Katherine Solace McKendrick stood on the crest of the hill and cupped her mouth with her hands.

"Jason!" she called, as loud as she could. "Jason McKendrick!"

She lowered her hands and scanned the heavily treed ravines carved in between ridges and grassy slopes that were as familiar to her as the back of her hand. The fading light was making it difficult to see now. A small boy could be swallowed up in the countryside. Swallowed up whole and not seen again for some time.

Where in the devil could he have gotten to? she wondered in utter frustration. He was so darned quick! And he thought nothing could really happen to him. He had that sense of invincibility that only a happy childhood could give. There were times when she almost wished he'd had a few close calls . . . just enough to give him a little respect for life . . . and a little respect for his mother's carefully stated warnings!

She smiled reluctantly as she remembered her own growing up. She'd never paid much attention either, she had to admit. That thought merely brought on an irritated frown. Her son had no business repeating his mother's mistakes!

"Jason!"

Her voice was echoed with silence, broken only by the sound of the wind softly rustling in the trees. There was a hint of winter in the air. There always was at this time of year in the Sierra.

If she didn't find him soon, he was going to start getting cold.

She pulled her shawl more tightly around her shoulders. At times like this she began to miss Seth. Without him to share the burden, it all fell on her.

No sense in thinking like that, Kate, my girl, she told herself unsympathetically. There's no point in feeling bad about things you can't change. Just concentrate on the things you can.

That was her philosophy and it had stood her in good stead for quite some time. She walked farther on, heading toward the creek that ran through their property. Jason loved to play down there during the summer. Maybe he'd be there. She hoped so.

And she hoped he'd be playing down there next summer as well. He would if she had anything to say about it, she vowed for the millionth time. She wasn't giving up the ranch without a fight!

"And we Katherine Solace McKendricks know how to fight!" she said aloud.

"Jason!" she shouted, this time with quite noticeable irritation.

"Coming!" cried a small, high-pitched voice from the shadowy crags below her.

A small boy scrambled up the grassy hill and hurtled toward her exuberantly.

"You found me! No fair!" he protested as he grabbed her skirts with both hands and threw himself against her. His face was a little grimy but the eyes were big and bright with mischief.

Kate sighed and pulled him up into her arms.

"You little rascal!" she exclaimed in exasperation. "How many times have I told you not to hide from me out here? It's too dangerous, Jason! Especially late in the day like this!"

His lower lip pushed out rebelliously at her chastising words.

"But, Mom . . ." he wailed protestingly.

"There's no 'but, Mom' about it," Kate said sternly. "We'd better get back before Grandpa sends the sheriff after us!"

Her teasing voice and affectionate hug soothed his wounded male ego, which was the biggest thing about Jason at the moment. At five years of age Jason fancied himself ready for everything, and he was continually trying to prove it to his thoroughly unimpressed mother.

She set him down and they half walked and half skipped back to the house.

But Jason was still angry at his mother's spoiling the hide-and-seek and then telling him he was too little to play in his favorite haunt late in the afternoon. So he decided to keep a secret . . . something just he would know about.

His fingers closed possessively over the magic stone he'd found. He looked obliquely at her and felt better. It was all his. His own treasure. His very own.

T. J. Walker's Friday night poker game was about to commence, if commence was the right word to use. People kind of eased in early in the evening, gradually increasing the noise level and cigarette smoke, until there was quite a press of bodies.

The regulars had showed up at Walker's card parlor and were ordering draft beer and homemade sandwiches with gusto, building up their strength and their nerve. Naturally, everyone had good nights and bad, but in the long run it was always T.J. who won the lion's share . . . of winnings and of women. . . . He was an insatiable consumer of both.

T.J. was in an expansive mood. He laughed and joked with lifelong friends and total strangers alike. His pockets were full and he was loaded for bear. Tonight was going to be special.

"Hey, everybody!" he shouted, pounding on a table to break through the din of conversation. "I've got a surprise tonight!"

Rejoinders of "Oh, yeah?" "What's that, T.J.?" and "What's up?" filled the air. Someone asked, "You gonna clean us all out before midnight tonight, T.J.?" and was met with a hail of complaints and loud guffaws.

"No," replied their magnanimous host with a smug grin. "You're safe from me tonight."

Someone asked if it was their wives he was aiming for. The laughter was a little more nervous, but everyone was out for a good time, so no offense was taken.

T.J. grinned even more broadly.

"Not that either. You all know I'm all for the straight and narrow!"

That disclaimer met with hoots and much ribald laughter. T.J. held up his hands, asking for a little quiet.

"Tonight is going to be a night to remember here in Still Waters," he announced proudly. "We're going to have a special guest. . . . I've invited a professional gambler to come play a few hands with me."

11

Someone mumbled that it was about time T.J. picked on someone besides the local sheep for fleecing. T.J. glowered momentarily at the speaker before continuing his explanation.

". . . I promised him a high-stakes game. . . . Of course you're all welcome to draw straws to sit in with us if you want. . . ."

The shuffling of feet was eloquent enough in the awkward silence that followed his heavy hint.

T.J. nodded his head and grinned knowingly at the crowd.

"I figured you'd need to think about it. That's okay. Take your time. We've got all evening, boys." He bent his head apologetically toward several women in the room. "You, too, ladies," he said genially. "You too!"

Kate McKendrick cleared the dinner dishes off of the table and stacked them on the kitchen counter.

"Anybody want another slice of pie?" she called out.

"No!" chorused the two diners as they pushed themselves away from the table.

"Jason, go finish picking up your toys," she said in as clear and as authoritative a voice as she could muster at the end of a very long and exhausting day.

To her amazement he cheerily shouted back an "Okay, Mom," and scooted off in the general direction of the biggest pile of playthings.

Kate sighed and shook her head. By the time he got there and saw all of his things again, he'd probably forget what he was supposed to do and start playing with them. She plunged her hands into dishwater up to her elbows and started washing up. She'd just have to worry about the toys later.

"Kate . . ."

The tall man standing in the doorway of the kitchen leaned on his cane and watched her in thoughtful concern. It was an expression she'd seen a lot in the past few years.

"Yes, Pop?" she responded, stacking the soapy dishes and draining the single sink in order to rinse them off.

He sighed and shook his head sorrowfully.

"I'm sorry for the way things have turned out for you, Kate," he said gravely. "This isn't the way you dreamed life would be, was it?"

She stared at the clear water as it rinsed away the suds, not wanting him to see her feelings at the moment. She had to be strong for them all. By force of will she managed to strangle her exhaustion and discouragement.

His question wasn't exactly unexpected. They'd been working up to this conversation for months now. Kate had done everything in her power to avoid it. She'd ignored his hints, his worried looks, his guilty comments. She'd been as cheerful and as stoic as she knew how to be. But she could tell from his stance and his tone of voice that this time they were going to talk about it. It brought a sinking feeling to the pit of her stomach.

"Pop . . ." she protested.

"Nope," he interrupted with a firm, dismissing wave of one gnarled hand. "After Seth died, I should have let you go . . . *told* you to go. You and Jason could have made a home near your folks in San Francisco. No matter how much you love it here, it would have been better for you and maybe for Jason too."

He spoke slowly, as if seeing the past five hard years with each word.

"You've got to face it, Kate. You need help to keep this place going. I'm too old to do what needs to be done. And with Walker wanting the land for himself, you're not likely to get much help from the folks around here."

He cleared his throat, trying to push down the emotions that boiled inside.

"I want you to consider leaving, Kate."

Her head jerked up and she stared at him in shock.

"This is my home," she whispered. "Our home. It's been part of me and I've been part of it for as long as I can remember."

He stabbed the floor with the tip of his cane.

"Don't you think I know that?" he countered angrily. "Do you think I would say this to you if I saw any way out?"

"Please, Pop. Just give me a little more time. I can take care of us."

The old man bowed his head and squeezed his eyes shut. Damnation! If he were only twenty or thirty years younger, he could help her. She needed a man. Whether she married one or just hired him, she needed muscle and brawn. And she was too stubborn to admit it!

"Katherine," he sighed in frustration. "How long do you think I can stand by and watch you struggle to keep a roof over our heads? I may not be able to run the spread anymore, but I'll be damned if I'll sit in my rocker and watch you brought to your knees tryin' to keep this place!"

She hung up the dish towel and turned to him, hands on hips.

"It isn't just for us, Pop," she reminded him with a challenging frown. "It's for Jason. This ranch will be his one day, like it was his father's and mine and yours and our people's for five generations back. I have to fight for it, Pop. And you have to let me try!"

They stared at each other across the room.

"Kate, you can't make it here without a man," he said forcefully, venting all his pent-up frustration on her.

She stubbornly stood her ground.

"I have to," she shot back. "I can and I will." Her eyes narrowed. "If you'll recall, Pop, it's been done before."

He glowered at her and leaned more heavily on his cane. She *would* have to bring that up, he thought in annoyance.

"That was different," he grumbled. "Things were different back then."

"Things were worse!"

Her father-in-law knew that he'd lost the battle. Invoking the memory of the first Katherine Solace McKendrick was dirty pool to his way of thinking. But his bad leg was beginning to feel numb and he couldn't think of anything else to say right now to try and convince her to give up. And deep in his heart, maybe he really didn't want her to.

Kate ran to him and hugged him fiercely.

"You can't chase me off that easily," she told him, as she led him back into the parlor. "Haven't you learned that by now?"

He leaned on his cane with one hand and on Kate with his other. Next to his late wife and his mother, he couldn't think of a woman he'd ever admired more.

"No, I guess not."

He squeezed her shoulder affectionately, but the deep sadness was still in his heart. She deserved better than this from life. Much better.

Matt Farrell stepped down out of the cab of the sixteen wheeler. A lightweight garment bag that had seen better days was slung casually over his shoulder.

"Thanks for the lift," he said, giving a nod of farewell to the potbellied driver. "Stay awake. And if you're ever in Reno, be sure and look me up. I owe you one, pal."

The driver grinned and patted the shirt pocket where he'd tucked Farrell's name and address.

"Sure thing, buddy! Good luck with the car!"

Farrell grimaced.

"Thanks," he said.

If he never saw another rented Ford, it would be too soon, he added to himself. Who in the hell needed to break down in the middle of the Sierra Nevada?

He watched the big truck roll down the road that led back to the nearby highway. Then he shifted the weight on his shoulder to a more comfortable position and started walking in the opposite direction. It had been a long time since he'd been in one of these little northern California towns. He'd steered clear of places with populations smaller than 75,000 for nearly all of his adult life. They held nothing but bitter memories for him.

Matt Farrell wanted nothing to do with them.

He was still not quite sure why he'd agreed to this game in Still Waters. Maybe curiosity . . . maybe a desire to exact a little repayment for past injuries . . . or maybe just to kill some time. How would he be treated now that he wasn't just some drifter's kid?

He grinned wryly. This wasn't exactly the way he'd envisioned arriving, of course! But that couldn't be helped now.

He climbed the steps of the diner next to the card parlor at the edge of town. The noise sounded the same as it did just about anyplace, he thought in amusement. Maybe little towns weren't so different after all . . . if you were an invited guest, that is.

The moment he stepped inside all eyes turned toward him and all conversation tapered off.

"Is there a T. J. Walker here?" Farrell inquired, scanning the assembly with a shrewd-eyed gaze.

A big man stepped forward, pushing through the crowd from the other room.

"I'm T. J. Walker," he boomed. "And you must be Matt Farrell! Right this way, Farrell," he said after shaking hands and clapping an arm around Farrell's shoulders. "How about something to drink before we sit down for a little game, huh?"

Farrell smiled slightly. Walker was exactly what he'd expected. He had the feeling it was going to be a long weekend. All in a good cause, Farrell, he reminded himself. All in a good cause.

Kate thought that weekend went much too fast. As usual there was more to do than there was time to do it in. By Sunday morning she found herself racing just to keep up with her schedule of things to attend to. She'd been too busy to hear about "the big game."

You could always tell Sunday morning in Still Waters. There was a reserved, proper kind of quiet that hung over the town. And everyone looked their spit-and-polish best.

"Good morning, Kate."

"Good morning, Mrs. Duncan."

Kate smiled, although it didn't come as easily with Mrs. Duncan as with most people she knew. Slim, nervous Mrs. Duncan stepped closer, looking sideways at Kate.

"Wasn't that a moving sermon?" she asked. Before Kate could misconstrue that as a real question, Mrs. Duncan hurried to make her point. "He must have heard about that poker game at T.J.'s!"

Mrs. Duncan pursed her lips disapprovingly and looked at Kate as if expecting her to reflect similar condemnation.

"What?" Kate murmured absently as they slowly made their way out of the small rural church with the rest of the tiny congregation.

"That part about not throwing your pearls before swine," she whispered righteously. "Don't you think he meant gambling? Especially with . . ." Her tone of voice and facial expression conveyed the depth of her distaste as she said, "Professional gamblers!" She squinted as they walked into the sunlight and shielded her eyes from the light as she looked at Kate.

"You know about T. J. Walker's Friday night poker game, of course?"

Kate smiled at several other departing acquaintances.

"No, Mrs. Duncan," she said dryly. "I'm afraid I don't."

The drawn woman exchanged her usual sour expression for a well-practiced look of civic outrage.

"Why, it's been going on all weekend! And it's still not done! That big-city gambler cleaned out several men. Of course they should have known better!" she snorted in disgust. "Even T.J. is losing this time. . . . And I hear he isn't taking it well at all. . . . His daddy'll put him on a short leash if he finds out!"

When Mrs. Duncan finally stopped to take a breath, Kate smiled at her as sweetly as she could manage and inquired, "Why, Mrs. Duncan, were you there for the past two days? It sounds ever so interesting. Tell me . . . did you play a hand or two yourself just for fun?"

Kate had the immense satisfaction of seeing the town gossip struck dumb. As Mrs. Duncan spluttered that she'd never even set foot in the wicked place, Kate was saved by the minister, who shook hands and pretended to be unaware of everything he'd just heard.

"How's the business coming along, Kate?" he asked with a genial smile.

Abigail Duncan turned her horrified face toward the people behind her and began regaling them with the same story that had been so unsatisfactorily received by Kate McKendrick. Since Mrs. Duncan was expert in corralling the attention of others, Kate and the minister were provided with a few minutes of fairly private conversation.

The privacy gave Kate room to speak honestly. She was grateful for that. Kate liked the Reverend Peter Vining. He was a warm, kindhearted, honest man. And he was a friend. At the moment that appeared to be a dwindling breed if not a downright endangered species.

"To be honest, Peter, I'm afraid I'm going to need some help," she admitted rather grudgingly. "Do you happen to know if anyone in Still Waters is looking for a few hours of work in the next couple of weeks? Someone who could work knowing I can't pay until the end of the month?"

Kate hated to ask. He knew she'd come to him only as a last

resort. It was a small town. It was never any secret who was looking for work and who wasn't. You asked the minister only when the normal channels weren't working. It had the odor of failure. Kate knew it. And so did Peter Vining.

He frowned. If he'd been inclined to swear, this would be one of the times he'd have uttered an expletive. Instead he just wondered once again why the Walkers were being so single-mindedly determined to bring this handsome young woman to her knees.

"No, Kate. I'm sorry. I don't," he replied slowly. "I'll be happy to ask around . . . very discreetly, I promise," he said under his breath. He put a sympathetic hand on her shoulder. "I can make a couple of calls to people outside Still Waters. . . ."

Kate forced a smile.

"Thanks, Peter. I'd appreciate that."

He nodded his head. They were standing a little closer together than most but hadn't realized it until Kate's instincts told her she was being watched. She glanced back and caught Abigail Duncan's rapt attention. The Reverend Mr. Vining noticed as well, and cleared his throat awkwardly. He couldn't afford any scandals, and he certainly wished to protect Kate from any more hardships.

"Good to see you this morning, Kate," he said quickly.

He turned his most charming smile on a surprised Abigail Duncan. Kate had never seen her look more radiant as, a few minutes later, she saw Abigail detailing some of her favorite reminiscences of life in Still Waters as a young girl, years ago. . . .

Kate was half laughing out loud as she walked toward home. She owed Peter Vining for his willingness to help, to say nothing of the smooth, tactful way he'd steered the spiteful Mrs. Duncan away from their appearance of intimate conversation. Maybe she'd invite their new minister to her house for supper one night by way of thanks. Wouldn't that just set Abigail Duncan's tongue to wagging! Wouldn't it just!

The following morning Loren McKendrick stood on the front porch of the house he'd grown up in and squinted at the gray shroud overhead. For seventy-two years he'd called this land home. He knew it as well as he knew himself. Maybe better.

"Looks like bad weather'll be comin' soon, Kate," he observed with fatalistic calm.

More than seven decades of living with Mother Nature had taught him to accept a great deal. Especially the things you couldn't change . . . if you were smart enough to tell what those things were.

She joined him on the porch and he patted her affectionately.

"Gonna see if you can find someone willing to stand up to T. J. Walker?" he asked, giving her a shrewd look with piercing black eyes undaunted by time.

"No harm in trying," she replied a little defensively. She'd certainly avoided it as long as possible. After last year she knew what the Walkers would do to anyone in Still Waters who helped her out.

"Nope," he agreed. "No harm in trying."

"You know, Pop, I think I've been pretty lucky over the years. I got everything I ever really wanted." She spoke softly, looking out over the darkened hills. "Some people just seem to be lucky like that, I think. I certainly never thought of myself as more deserving than the next person."

She started down the steps and whistled sharply. A big, black dog bounded out from in back of the barn and loped across the open space until he reached her feet. She bent down and rubbed his ears.

The sun had been up for a couple of hours, but the cloud cover made it seem more like the end of the day.

"I'll be back as soon as I can, Pop," she called out as she headed down the dirt road that led toward town.

"Right," he called back gruffly. Then, to himself, he added, "I sure hope your luck holds."

Kate had decided not to wait to hear from Peter Vining. Monday morning was as good a day as any to start making some inquiries on her own. Besides, she could do her asking while she was taking care of a little grocery shopping. That ought to keep people off the scent for a while.

The Still Waters General Store sold just about everything.

"Morning, Kate," called out the jovial red-cheeked woman behind the counter.

"Hi, Jerico," Kate returned as she closed the door behind her.

Jerico Johnson was one of Kate's favorite people. She was down to earth, warm, and friendly. She was the kind of person who'd give you the shirt off her back if she thought you needed it more than she did. She was also one of the few people left in Still Waters whom Kate could approach for help. Jerico Johnson was a friend indeed.

"Need something special today, Kate?" Jerico called out as she put some cans up on the shelf behind the counter.

Kate needed something special all right, but it didn't come on a shelf.

"You could say that."

"What're you lookin' for?" Jerico asked, turning to study Kate a little more closely. It wasn't like Kate to hang back, as if she were searching for the words.

"Well . . ." Out with it, Kate ordered herself. "I was wondering if you knew of anyone looking for a job around here?"

Kate's eyes never wavered, but Jerico's did.

"Oh, Kate," Jerico sighed, pressing her lips together. "I wish I could come out there and help you myself," she said regretfully.

Kate gave her friend a comforting smile and shook her head, waving off the concern. She looked over Jerico's shoulder and checked the community message board behind the counter. There were a few notes, hand-scrawled, here and there.

Jerico saw the direction of her gaze.

"There are one or two about doing odd jobs," she admitted. "But they made a point of telling me they wouldn't work at your spread." Jerico's soft face hardened in exasperation and disgust. "What are these men around here made of?"

Kate laughed humorlessly.

"Most of them have a lot of mouths to feed and no way of doing that if the Walkers decide to call in their debts," she reminded Jerico.

Jerico grumbled unsympathetically.

Kate made her way around the store, picking up enough things to fill a single grocery bag. When Kate was paying the bill Jerico slipped in a half-dozen freshly baked cinnamon buns, insisting they were for her favorite little "friend of the family" and there wasn't any charge.

"Thanks, Jerico," Kate said as she lifted the bag and opened the door.

Jerico wished her luck, but the look in her eyes as she watched Kate leave was not hopeful.

Still Waters was a small town. It took Kate all of five minutes to walk from Johnson's General Store at one end of it to the Sheriff's Office at the other. When she was passing by on her way home, the sheriff stepped onto his front porch and hailed her.

Kate debated the plausibility of pretending she hadn't heard. Since he wasn't that far away, she decided she'd have to be deaf not to have heard him. Reluctantly, she acknowledged his greeting. He jumped down the steps to the street and grabbed her by the elbow. There was a threatening growl from the black dog that had pushed between them. The sheriff dropped her arm and jumped back nervously.

"Hey, Kate, call him off!" he pleaded, reddening with embarrassment. "That's the damnedest dog you've got! Doesn't he ever make friends with anybody?" he complained.

Kate patted her side and the dog obligingly came around.

"Just with family, Vern."

He eyed the dog, then stepped toward his office, waving her in the same direction, though careful not to touch her this time.

"I haven't talked to you in a long time, Kate. Come on in. Have a cup of coffee with me."

Kate had opened her mouth to say no when she caught sight of T. J. Walker's pickup truck pulling into town. If she stood outside or continued up the street, he'd be sure to stop and talk to her. She wasn't interested in seeing him. She was so mad right now, she was afraid she'd say something she'd regret. When she had her showdown with T.J., she wanted to be holding a stronger hand than she had at the moment.

Vern Peterson was one surprised man when she smiled at him and said, "Why, thanks. That sounds just great."

The coffee was about the worst she'd ever had.

"Sorry about that," he said sheepishly. "It's been keeping warm all night. I guess I really didn't think you'd come in or I wouldn't even have offered it."

21

"Have a busy night?" she inquired, looking over the bare little office. Still Waters wasn't exactly known for problems with crime.

"Yeah. I was called over to the main highway to help some of the county boys out. Then when I got back I found some stranger wandering around as drunk as a skunk and causing quite a ruckus. Brought him back here to sleep it off."

Kate nodded. That was about Still Waters's speed, she thought. She eyed Vern thoughtfully. Well, at this point, there wasn't much to lose in asking. . . .

"Tell me, Vern," she began, running a finger over the edge of the cracked mug in her hand, "would you be interested in doing some extra work?"

He looked at her in surprise. Then a dull, ruddy color tinged his cheek.

"For you?" he asked guardedly.

She nodded.

He stood up and walked around the desk, then paced slowly around the room, considering. . . . Finally he stopped and turned to face her. He looked her steadily in the eyes.

"I'm sorry, Kate. I can't do it." He licked his lips, then plunged on. "I'd be putting my own place . . . and my brothers' . . . on the line if I did. And what for?" There was a challenging flare in his eyes as he remembered the times he'd tried to court her over the years, only to be rebuffed. "But if you sell out, and need a place to stay . . . I'd always take you in, Kate. You and the boy. And the old man, for that matter."

His expression hardened.

"I'd do that for you . . . for a wife, Kate," he added bluntly, so there could be no misunderstanding. "But to stand in T.J.'s line of fire just for the pleasure of your company? No, Kate. That's not good enough."

Kate put down the mug.

At least Vern was honest and straightforward about it, she thought. Unlike a lot of others in town.

"Thanks for the coffee, Vern," she said, turning as if to go.

A dull clanking of metal from the cell block attached to the back of the office attracted their attention. The sound of a cage being rattled.

"Hey!" The muffled growl sounded like it belonged to a very

irritated man. "Are you going to socialize all day? I want to see the sheriff!"

Vern reached for his keys. Kate stopped in her tracks.

"Who's that?" she asked.

"The drunk from last night that I told you about."

As Peterson unlocked the door and stepped into the cell block, an idea formed in Kate's mind. She quietly followed him inside.

Matt Farrell was holding his head with one hand and the iron bar in front of him with the other. He felt like he'd been run over by a freight train, clobbered with a blackjack, and dumped on a bed of rocks to sleep off his ill fortune. He was not in the mood to listen to the sheriff chat with his lady love. He wanted out. And he wanted it now.

"Well, how are you feeling?" asked the sheriff, giving his prisoner the once-over as he approached the cell.

The prisoner looked at the two people entering his small chambers and scowled.

"Like hell," he snarled. "Why the hell am I in jail? I was the victim, not the criminal!"

Peterson looked at him in great surprise.

"Is that so?" he asked disbelievingly. "Then maybe you could explain why I found you staggering around Still Waters falling down drunk . . . alone . . . last night?"

"I wasn't drunk, Sheriff," Farrell retorted angrily. "One of your fine, upstanding citizens slipped me a Mickey Finn and then proceeded to rob me."

Peterson looked startled at first, then he began to laugh.

"And who did this, if you don't mind my asking?" inquired the clearly dubious sheriff.

Farrell's eyes narrowed dangerously.

"A man by the name of T. J. Walker. You know him, I imagine."

"You imagine right." Peterson looked the prisoner over. "Just about everyone around here knows T.J. But I don't think I've ever had the honor of making your acquaintance," he pointed out with undisguised sarcasm.

Farrell certainly didn't look like anyone worth knowing. His clothes were dirty and torn. His face was bruised and scratched.

23

He smelled like he'd fallen into a garbage can at some point in his bender.

He was so mad and felt so lousy, however, that he couldn't have cared less.

"The name's Farrell, Matt Farrell."

That caused both Peterson and Kate to blink. The name had been the only interesting new piece of conversation all weekend.

"You're the gambler who came to town to play poker with T.J.?" Kate asked in surprise.

Farrell gave her a quick, assessing look.

"Yes."

Peterson turned on Kate in surprise. He hadn't been aware she'd followed him into the cell block.

"You shouldn't be in here, Kate," he said disapprovingly.

"Well, I already am," Kate pointed out, stepping a little farther inside to silence his objection.

Kate felt the imprisoned man's gaze boring into her. She wasn't the type to flinch under a man's scrutiny; she was well accustomed to holding her own with men, both socially and in managing the ranch.

There was something vaguely unsettling about Farrell's penetrating scrutiny, however. Underneath his scruffy appearance lay a different man altogether, she was sure.

She stared back at him, forcing the nagging feeling of disquiet into oblivion. Don't get sidetracked, Kate, she told herself. You've got enough to handle already!

"Look, Sheriff," Farrell said coldly. "If you're going to hold me, I have the right to make a phone call. If you're not going to, I'd appreciate it if you'd let me out of here."

Kate and Peterson both heard the rest of what he was thinking as clearly as if he had said it. He had some unfinished business to take care of in Still Waters. And he wanted to get on with it.

Peterson didn't want any trouble. He had a nice life here . . . ranching part-time . . . working as the town sheriff part-time . . . but he could take one look at Matt Farrell and see nothing but problems as long as the man was in town. He wanted him gone. Gamblers weren't like the rest of them. The people around here were hardworking, honest folks. If T.J. and some of the boys had gotten a little carried away . . . well . . .

"The charges are drunk and disorderly. Vagrancy. Being found in an intoxicated condition within the town limits."

Farrell's face froze. So that's the way it's going to be, he thought. Well, it sure wouldn't be the first time "good" local people had tried to railroad him. He knew how to handle that, all right. He was about to say he'd make his phone call when the woman spoke again.

"How much is his fine?" she asked evenly.

Peterson looked at her in shock. Farrell, although taken by surprise, didn't show it. He merely took a closer look. It didn't explain much.

"You can't . . ." blustered the sheriff.

"Do you need a place to stay, something to eat, and a week or two to get in touch with friends or figure out what you're going to do next, Mr. Farrell?" she asked, directing herself for the first time to him.

Admiration flickered in his dark eyes. She was one spunky lady. But she had an angle somewhere and he didn't know what it was. On the other hand, he reminded himself, he wasn't in a very strong position to bargain from right now. Beggars couldn't be choosers. . . .

"As a matter of fact, ma'am, I do."

"For all you know, Kate, this man could be a dangerous criminal!" protested Peterson, visibly upset by her offer.

"Have you checked to see if he's wanted, Vern?" she asked patiently.

Somehow, she didn't think Farrell was a criminal. The man staring at her, though beaten up and in bad shape at the moment, looked too smart, too successful to be a common criminal. Dangerous, maybe . . . she had to admit that.

"Not yet . . . I just found out who he was."

"Well, if you find anything, Vern, you can come on out and pick him up," she said reasonably. "I think we can take care of ourselves until then."

The sheriff started sputtering objections. None of them sounded like they could stand up to legal scrutiny, however, so he turned toward the prisoner.

"Do you want to go with Mrs. McKendrick?" he asked challengingly.

"Room, board, and two weeks at your place . . . in exchange for what?" Farrell asked bluntly.

"Eight hours a day of work around the ranch. Hard, physical work." She gave him a doubtful look, wondering if he'd be strong enough to do anything. He didn't look like he was in very good shape right now.

Farrell grinned faintly. He didn't look particularly amused, however.

"I can handle that all right," he said. "Do you think you could give me today to get over the shanghaiing your noble town folks administered?" he asked with soft sarcasm.

Her eyes blazed defensively.

"Of course, Mr. Farrell. We'll even throw in free health care. No extra charge."

He nodded his head in acknowledgment, raising an eyebrow in amusement at her spirit.

She turned on the sheriff.

"Is there anything I need to sign?" she asked.

Peterson swore under his breath and unlocked the cell.

"No. I'll hold the paperwork. If there are no problems while he's at your place"—he gave Farrell a warning look—"and I don't hear of any outstanding charges, we'll just forget the whole thing when he leaves town."

CHAPTER TWO

Samuel Walker, who had just returned from a banking convention, sat down at the well-appointed dining-room table and tucked his napkin under his chin. It was a habit of many years that he indulged himself in only when dining at home. It made him feel like the common man his father had been. Common except for the family tendency for personal ambition, of course.

"You're late," he said, raising his fork to his mouth and not so much as glancing at the man dressed in outdoor clothes who'd just entered. He knew without looking who it was. Where his son T.J. was concerned, his paternal radar was never wrong.

"Wouldn't want to spoil my record, Major," his son drawled as he pulled up a chair and sat down across the table.

The cook brought in another dish and set it in front of T.J. Neither of the men spoke until she'd left and the sound of her footsteps had faded into the kitchen down the hall.

"I hear there was some excitement last weekend while I was in Los Angeles," the older man observed, carefully carving up the steak on his plate.

T.J. grunted and stuffed his mouth with potatoes.

The elder Walker gave his son to the count of ten. When no more explanations were forthcoming he laid down his knife and fork and stared long and hard at the full-grown man who persisted in behaving like an adolescent boy half of the time.

"Are you going to tell me or am I going to have to drag it out of you . . . one admission at a time?"

T.J. frowned at his plate and reached for the cold beer in front of him. He took a long swallow and wiped his mouth with the back of his sleeve before replying. He was sick and tired of his old man browbeating him every time he kicked up his heels

27

a little. Much as T.J. admired and respected him, he sometimes intensely disliked his father.

T.J. wanted to be the top man around Still Waters. The undisputed, uncontested top dog. And as long as his eagle-eyed, tightfisted father refused to turn over the reins of local power to him, that dream was unlikely to be realized.

"We had a professional cardsharp come to liven things up a little at the card parlor Friday night." T.J. reached for some chili peppers and ladled them onto his plate. He didn't look at his suspicious father, who was still staring at him in a very unsympathetic way. "We got pretty well taken to the cleaners. When he left town on Sunday night nobody was too sad to see him go."

The senior Walker watched impatiently as his son began eating steak and chili peppers with obvious relish. As T.J. reached for some cold beer to put out the fire in his mouth, his father thumped his hand on the table.

"That wasn't the end of it, the way I hear it!" the older man said angrily.

"Who says?" T.J. asked with a challenging look. He liked to know who his father's sources were on occasions like this. Once he found out, he'd see to it they didn't leak news ever again.

However, his father hadn't acquired the local reins of power out of a mere stroke of good luck. As softhearted as he was for his son, he was not stupid.

"The way I heard it," went on the older man, "your highrolling guest had an unfortunate mishap on his way out of town."

T.J. raised his eyebrows in imitation surprise.

"Oh, yeah?" he said insincerely. "Say, that's too bad. I'm real sorry to hear it."

Sam Walker frowned even more. His face was reddening in anger.

"T.J.," he said, leaning forward and giving his wayward offspring a venomous look. "I want all this crap to stop! I want no more wild cowboy high jinks, no more drunken pranks, no more wasting our hard-earned money on cheap women and gambling!"

T.J. sat stiffly in his chair, glaring rebelliously as his father

28

paused for effect. The next words the older man uttered were not exactly unexpected.

"I want you to get married, settle down, and have some kids!" Samuel Walker said as clearly and as loudly as possible without raising the household. "I want to see my grandchildren before I leave this earth, damn it!"

T.J. was saved from having to respond right away when the cook reappeared to clear the table and serve coffee.

"And I don't mean bastards . . . or brats from that Wells woman!" the elder Walker finished the minute they were alone again.

T.J. tossed down his napkin and shoved back his chair. As he rose angrily to his feet, he looked down at his father in stony defiance.

"I'm not a boy anymore, Major. I'm a man. And I'll do as I please, when I please, with whom I please. If and when I take a wife, *I'll* choose her . . . and *I'll* decide when it's time to father some kids . . . without any help from you!"

He stalked out of the room, brushing past the very surprised foreman who had been standing outside the dining-room door, hat in hand, about to knock.

"Should I come back later, Mr. Walker?" the foreman inquired in embarrassment.

Samuel shook his head and motioned for the man to enter.

"No, Clint. Come on in. T.J. and I appear to be finished . . . for the moment." He tried to tamp down his anger at his only son's infuriating refusal to grow up and turned his attention to his foreman. "What can I do for you?"

"It's about the assay report you wanted, Mr. Walker. It was delivered to me this morning." The foreman pulled a long envelope from the inside of his jacket and handed it to his boss. "I know you wanted to see it as soon as it arrived."

Walker took it from him and ripped it open. A strange light filled his narrowed eyes. He looked up at his foreman abruptly.

"No one else knows about this report?"

"That's right, sir. We did it all just the way you told us to."

Walker folded up the paper and slid it back into the envelope.

"Thanks, Clint. I'll see to it your paycheck has a bonus in it."

"Yessir, Mr. Walker. Thank you."

29

It was well past noon when Kate and Farrell got back to the McKendrick ranch. When Loren McKendrick saw them walking up the lane he didn't quite know what to make of it.

Matt Farrell wasn't quite sure what to make of it either. He'd walked up the winding dirt road that led to the McKendrick place, wondering each step of the way whether he'd made a mistake in accepting Kate's offer in his haste to get out of jail. Every inch of his body ached from the beating he'd taken, but he was too stubborn to admit it. By the time they reached the front porch he wasn't sure he could climb the steps.

But he'd never tell Kate that!

After the one long, cool look she'd given him at the jail, she'd appeared to have forgotten he was even with her. They'd walked for forty minutes in silence.

At least she'd carried her own bag, he thought in disgust. Falling down because he was too weak to carry a bag of food up a hill was all he needed! He felt enough of a fool as it was. He hadn't been jumped like that since he was a kid.

The black dog that had walked between Kate and Farrell growled warningly as Farrell started up the first step. Farrell eyed the dog and stopped, one foot on the step and the other on the ground.

"I think your dog's trying to tell me something," Farrell said evenly.

"Doc!" Kate ordered without giving either of them a glance. "Heel!"

Immediately the dog bounded up the steps after her, keeping close to her side.

"Farrell, this is my father-in-law, Loren McKendrick," she called out over her shoulder. "Pop, this is Matt Farrell. Mr. Farrell will be working for us for a couple of weeks."

The two men stared at each other and gruffly shook hands. Kate had swept on into the kitchen and left them to complete their introductions on their own. The sound of thunder and a brilliant streak of lightning shortened the awkward situation for them.

"Better get inside before we get soaked," McKendrick observed as big drops of rain began splashing down onto the dirt.

"Thanks," Farrell replied stonily, trying to convince himself that every step up did not send streaks of pain shooting through

30

his legs and that he wasn't going to fall flat on his face any second now.

"You can wash up down there," McKendrick said, pointing toward a hallway.

While Farrell followed McKendrick's suggestion Loren joined his daughter-in-law in the kitchen, where she was just finishing putting away the groceries she'd bought.

"Where in God's green earth did you find that smelly, broken-down, beaten-up drunk, Kate?" he bellowed in astonishment.

Her father-in-law's prosaic description reminded Kate of something she'd intended to do.

"In jail," she replied succinctly as she hurried out of the kitchen.

She unearthed a couple of old towels and a fresh bar of soap. Then she knocked on the bathroom door.

It sounded like the house was falling down to Farrell. He gripped his painfully throbbing head and flung open the door.

"Don't do that!" he thundered, instantly regretting his own loudness and shutting his eyes in agony.

He'd unbuttoned his shirt and had been washing his face. Kate studied his dripping features and wondered how he'd ended up in this kind of a fix. He wasn't too bad-looking, she realized for the first time.

She blinked her eyes and forced that thought into the recesses of her mind. There was absolutely no purpose in becoming too friendly with the man, she told herself. She had enough problems as it was. She didn't need to start feeling sorry for a broken-down gambler! He was a big boy. He'd have to solve his own problems.

"Sorry, Mr. Farrell," she said, politely apologetic. "I thought you might like to get cleaned up, so I brought you some towels and soap. Feel free to take as much time as you need. Lunch will be ready in half an hour or so, but we'll keep it warm for you. Come when you're ready."

He dropped one hand slowly to his side and looked at her. She came up to his cheekbones, he noticed in surprise. She was kind of a slender little thing up close. Walking next to her and listening to her stand down the sheriff had made her seem six feet tall somehow. A slow glimmer of amusement at his own obtuseness began to surface in his eyes.

He found himself wondering what it would have been like to have met her under different circumstances. If a mutual friend had introduced them at a restaurant, say . . . and he'd spent an evening with her, getting acquainted . . . He brought his imagination to a sharp stop. They hadn't met like that. That wasn't the way things were going to be between them, he told himself bluntly. And yet . . . the image of her smiling face kept floating there in his mind for a bit . . . It was hard to let go of. Very hard.

"Thanks, ma'am," he replied politely.

She turned to go, then hesitated, not quite sure whether to say what she was thinking or not. He would smell a lot better if he had a change of clothes, she told herself. Offering him clothing did not come easily to her. The only clothes she had to offer were Seth's. Letting him wear Seth's clothes was almost like offering him friendship. She didn't want to offer Farrell friendship. She wanted him to work for her for the next two weeks.

She got another whiff of his clothing about then. That settled the debate. She turned to him and looked him over with a critical eye.

"I don't suppose you have a change of clothes?" she asked dubiously.

Farrell was tempted to laugh, but he refrained. His head couldn't take laughter quite yet.

"I did. But whoever decided to use me as a punching bag must have decided to take them off my hands."

She nodded. Not that she completely believed him. She couldn't remember the last time anyone had been attacked in Still Waters. Maybe he was an alcoholic and the "attackers" were just a part of his drunken hallucinations. But he obviously didn't have anything else to wear at the moment.

"I have some things that will probably fit. You can give me your things to wash."

She walked away without waiting for his reply. When she returned with the clothes he gave her a mildly surprised thanks. Farrell had been a stranger in any number of towns over the years. But he'd never met anyone quite like Kate McKendrick before. He wondered whose clothes she had given him. And he wondered for the first time where her husband was. No one had mentioned her husband. No one at all.

By the time Farrell got to the dining-room table, Kate was pouring a last cup of tea for herself. He sat down at the place set for him just as a small whirlwind rounded the corner. Jason climbed up onto his chair and studied Farrell with open curiosity.

"Jason, this is Mr. Farrell. He'll be working for us for the next couple of weeks," his mother explained. "This is my son, Jason," she added for Farrell's benefit.

"Hello, Jason," Farrell said politely just before digging into the homemade vegetable soup in front of him.

"Why's he gonna be here?" Jason asked with a childish frown.

"We need some help with the fences and the repairs on the barn," his mother replied as she wiped some jam off his face.

No matter how often she cleaned him up, the next time she saw Jason he always managed to have gotten messy again. Everyone she knew said boys were just like that. Kate glanced at Farrell's battered face and wondered if they ever outgrew the tendency.

"But *I* was doing that!" Jason wailed in dismay. "I was helping you! You said I did good, Mommy!"

Kate looked at Jason in exasperation.

"You did very well, Jason. And we'll fix some other things . . . you and I. But we've got so much to fix, Grandpa and I decided to hire someone to help us out."

Farrell was savoring the delicious flavor of the soup and watching the interchange curiously. From the scowling glare Jason gave him just before scampering out of the room, Farrell had the feeling the issue was not settled yet. It was just a matter of time before Jason tried to get around his mother's edict, Farrell decided. He was so sure of that, he'd have bet on it.

It took only one day for Farrell to be proved correct.

"Here," Jason blurted out the following afternoon.

Farrell looked down from the ladder he was standing on to see a small face looking up at him, a nail held in a tiny, outstretched hand.

Matt reached down and took the offering with a grunt of

33

thanks. He hammered it into the wall and immediately received another from his half-pint assistant.

"I used to help Mom like this," Jason said proudly.

Matt didn't miss a stroke. The hammer fell smoothly against the nailhead again and again.

"That so?"

"Yeah," Jason said. "You're almost as good as her," he added, trying to be complimentary. Jason couldn't quite figure out how to approach the taciturn stranger his mother was putting up in the old homestead in back of the barn, but he figured anyone would be proud to be told he could nail almost as well as she could.

Farrell stopped in mid-stroke and looked down, nonplussed.

"Is that so?" he asked. Farrell had never met a woman who could hammer a nail straight and for the moment he wasn't quite sure how to answer. One look at the earnest little face helped clarify that. "Thanks," he said with a grin as he took another nail from his helper.

He was feeling almost human today. Kate's food, blankets, and a sound night's sleep had helped heal the worst of his injuries. Only a few aches and pains remained . . . many of them in his pride.

"Where is your mom anyway? I haven't seen her since breakfast."

"Oh, she had to go out to check the cattle. She should be back after lunch. She promised we'd play hide-and-seek this afternoon."

Farrell smiled as he finished the section he'd been working on all morning. Riding herd on cattle in the morning and playing with her kid in the afternoon . . . that had to be an exhausting way to live.

Farrell was about to ask Jason whether it was always like this when the sound of an approaching pickup truck interrupted them.

"Kate! Kate McKendrick!" boomed an eager, confident male voice.

It was a voice Farrell recognized immediately. He put down the hammer and began stepping down the ladder, his jaw tight with anger.

"Mom's out in the north section," Jason cried as he ran

through the open doors of the barn at full tilt. It was always exciting when someone came to call as far as Jason was concerned.

By the time Farrell reached the doors, which were flung wide open, the sound of approaching hoofbeats announced Kate's return. She rode up to the barn, walking the last part and hailing her son and their visitor as she drew near.

"Hi, Jason! Hello, T.J.," she called out to them.

Did she sound a little stiff with Walker or was it just his imagination, Farrell wondered as he stood in the shadowy entrance and watched her dismount.

"What are you doing out here, T.J.?" Kate asked easily as she loosened the cinch and began cooling her horse.

T.J. was struggling to hold on to Jason, whom he'd picked up and swung onto one shoulder when the little boy had hurtled toward him earlier.

"Just bein' neighborly, Kate," he drawled with a charming, if transparently superficial, grin. "Thought I'd see if you needed any help . . . bein' a woman alone . . . and a longtime friend."

Jason managed to squirm out onto one arm so far that T.J. had to let go or be toppled over from being off balance. He ran to his mother and took the reins from her.

"Can I do it, Mom? I can do it! Please . . ."

Kate smiled at him and tousled his curly blond hair.

"Sure, honey. Why don't you walk her around the corral for a few minutes, till she feels cool." Kate watched fondly as her three-and-a-half-foot son walked her eight-hundred-pound quarter horse off toward the designated cooling area. She was a good mare, docile and intelligent . . . and Jason already was showing a knack for handling animals . . . no matter how much bigger they were than he was!

"You've done a good job with the boy, Kate," T.J. said with sincere praise. "You've done a good job with the ranch . . . with everything."

Kate turned back to look at the big man in front of her.

"Thanks, T.J." She eyed him coolly. "Is that why you drove out here today? To tell me what a good job I'm doing?"

T.J. grinned at her . . . a boyish grin, intended to charm her out of her defensiveness and anger. It didn't work.

"Not at all, Kate, my girl," he drawled. "I wanted to offer to help you out, honey."

"Now just how would you do that, T.J.?" she asked curiously, walking toward his jeep in slow, measured steps.

"Well . . . I could send some boys over to help you with the cattle every once in a while . . ."

She stopped and rested a hand on the door, waiting for the rest.

"Or . . . I could offer to buy some land from you," he said, walking up behind her and laying a hand next to hers on the door.

"Or?" Kate prompted him, turning to look up at him. Her cool, green eyes never wavered in spite of the intentness of Walker's gaze.

"Or I could see to it that you could sell your cattle again . . . build whatever that thing is you're building . . . and had some help whenever you and Loren needed it."

His hot breath scorched her cheek. Kate thought for a moment she'd slap the man for his audacity. If she slapped him, though, she'd be losing control. And Kate wanted to keep a clear mind where this snake was concerned.

"And what do you get in return for all this neighborliness, T.J.?" she asked evenly.

He bowed and moved a little away from her.

"Your gratitude, Kate." But his eyes said something else. It made Kate's stomach curdle.

T.J. caught sight of Loren McKendrick, who was walking stiffly across the grass, leaning heavily on his cane. Both Kate and her father-in-law saw the condescension and pity in T.J.'s eyes. They both bristled at almost the same moment.

"Afternoon, T.J.," McKendrick said, not bothering with the "good," since it so obviously wasn't.

T.J. tipped his hat.

"Loren," he acknowledged. "I was just trying to make Kate an offer she couldn't refuse," he said, underlining his comment with a suggestive glance at Kate.

McKendrick did not look impressed. He stabbed the ground in front of him with the tip of his cane and leaned on it with both hands.

"I thought you'd learned, T.J.," McKendrick growled.

T.J.'s stance stiffened defensively.

"Learned what?" he asked, daring the old man to insult him. McKendrick didn't hesitate.

"You don't have anything she wants, T.J. And you never will."

T.J. took a menacing step forward, stopping abruptly when Kate moved in front of him, blocking his way.

"Watch your tongue, old man," he warned angrily. "You haven't been the top man around here for a long time." He surveyed the apron tied around Loren's waist and sneered, "And you don't look like that's gonna change, old woman!"

Kate felt Loren's anger without looking at him. She retaliated before her father-in-law had a chance. Her palm connected with T.J.'s cheek. She'd put her weight behind it and he staggered back a step, leaping forward almost immediately to grab her. Kate took a half step to the side and stuck out her foot. T.J.'s momentum had carried him too far, too fast. When he saw her boot he was already falling, face-first, into the ground.

"Good shot," McKendrick cackled with a dry laugh.

Walker struggled to get off of the damp ground, rubbing some mud from his slacks on the way up. It was then he finally noticed Farrell, who was leaning against the barn casually observing the play-by-play unfolding on the grassy mound.

After a moment of total speechlessness, T.J. gulped and swore unpleasantly. He turned his fury on Kate.

"What's Farrell doin' here, Kate?"

Kate glanced at Farrell, wondering how anyone could be so cool and removed. She reminded herself he was a drifter; he didn't know how to connect with people. Even so, she found herself annoyed at his detachment.

"He's working for us," she said shortly. "Now . . . get off our land, T.J.," she ordered coldly.

T.J. reached out and grabbed her by the forearm. It happened so fast, Kate hadn't had time to jump out of his reach. As it turned out, it didn't really matter. A furious black ball of fur hurtled toward them from the direction Jason had taken.

T.J. howled in pain and released Kate, concentrating on beating off the attacking dog.

"Get him off me or I'll have him killed!" T.J. screamed.

"Down, Doc!" Kate ordered. Reluctantly, and snarling his

reticence every step of the way, Doc obeyed. He stood stiff-legged between Kate and T.J., his eyes fixed on the big man rubbing the torn sleeve of his jacket.

"Lucky I wasn't in my shirt sleeves, Kate!" T.J. complained, keeping his eye on the dog as he got back into his truck. "He's crazy! Somebody in this town's gonna shoot him one of these days . . ."

Kate ran forward and slammed her hands against the open window frame.

"If Doc so much as develops a limp, T.J., I'll hold you responsible!"

Farrell watched the heated exchange with no outward show of interest. That came from a lifetime of practice, capped by a poker professional's discipline. But his thoughts were anything but detached. He was thinking what a lucky kid Jason was to have a mother like Kate . . . what a lucky man Loren McKendrick was to have her for a daughter-in-law. She was strong and had the nerve to stand up for herself and the people she loved. You didn't find many people like that anymore. Maybe you never had, he thought.

T.J. turned his narrow-eyed hostility toward the man leaning against the McKendrick's barn.

"Your luck isn't going to be any better here than it was in town, Farrell," T.J. warned loudly. "If I were you, I'd leave." He added significantly, "Just as soon as I could."

Kate watched Farrell nod impassively, wondering how a man could tolerate being ordered about like that. It must have showed on her face because for a moment her eyes locked with Farrell's and she felt as though he were touching her mind. A trickle of awareness ran down her spine.

"Thanks for the advice," Farrell said amiably, turning his attention back to T.J.

T.J. glared at the dog, which was still poised for action, the hair standing up on the back of its shoulders, ready to fight. He jerked the key, and the engine roared to life. Tires spun. He gunned the rattling vehicle down the dirt road full-tilt, banging hard over every rut.

Kate rubbed Doc's ears.

"Thanks, Doc," she murmured affectionately. She put her arms around his furry neck and hugged him.

Farrell watched and wondered what it would feel like to be in Doc's place. Then he told himself to stop thinking like that. He couldn't afford to get mixed up with a woman like Kate Mc-Kendrick. No, sir! She was trouble if he'd ever seen it. And he was *not* going to get into that kind of trouble!

Then suddenly she was standing and frowning in his direction. Before he could think of someplace he urgently needed to escape to, she was marching purposefully toward him.

"Well, Mr. Farrell, did T.J. convince you?" she demanded, every inch of her daring him to admit it only at risk of great bodily harm . . . from her.

Farrell backed into the barn, shaking his head in the negative.

"No, ma'am." Then he realized he hadn't the foggiest idea what the question was. He looked at her blankly and muttered, "Convince me of what?"

She backed him up against a stall, where he was forced to halt.

"To leave town as soon as possible," she explained impatiently.

When he simply stared at her with a perplexed look on his face, she began tapping her booted toe on the ground in irritation.

"Look, Mr. Farrell, just because you're a stranger here does not mean you have to be a whipping boy for someone like T. J. Walker," she said heatedly. "He has no right to threaten you or tell you what to do . . . none whatsoever."

Farrell was giving her a peculiar look. Kate decided he had probably never thought of his rights to anything and plunged on.

"Don't let him chase you off! Stand up to him. . . . Stay until you're darned good and ready to leave!"

Kate wasn't sure herself why she was so upset at the way T.J. had treated Farrell. She was even less clear about why it bothered her that Farrell had seemed to just stand there and accept the ultimatum that was being handed to him. And now that they were alone together in the relative darkness of the barn, she was becoming even more confused. All of a sudden she couldn't remember what her point had been. She found herself staring at this very disturbing stranger who now had his back against a stall. Why was it that *she* was beginning to feel cornered?

"Whatever you say, ma'am," Farrell muttered, clearing his throat in the middle of his reply.

She blinked quickly in surprise.

"You mean you're not leaving?" she asked in surprise.

"Not yet . . . that is, as long as we still have an agreement . . ."

"Oh, yes," she said quickly. She was surprised at how relieved she felt. She told herself it was strictly because they needed the help and it was Farrell or no one at this point.

Farrell finally realized he had an opportunity to find out exactly what was in it for Kate if he continued to work for her. He wasted no more time in putting the question to her.

"Tell me, Mrs. McKendrick," he asked curiously, "do you usually get your hired hands from the town jail?"

"No. You're a first."

Just as he was about to follow up on that, a small tornado blew into the barn shouting, "Mom! Calamity's cooled! Now what can I do?"

Kate turned away and took her noisy offspring toward the house. Farrell watched them go without comment. He kept busy the rest of the afternoon working on the repairs to the barn. When he went up for lunch only Loren was in the house. Farrell managed to resist the temptation of asking where Kate and Jason had gone.

Every night Farrell fell into bed feeling more exhausted than he had in years. He made one phone call the second day he was at the McKendricks'. Unfortunately, the person he was trying to reach wasn't in. Farrell left a brief explanation on the answering machine and turned his attention toward planning his strategy with T. J. Walker.

Whenever Kate and he had to talk he was polite but careful to keep his distance. Since Kate didn't seem interested in spending much time with him either, by the end of the first week neither of them knew much more about the other than they had at the end of the first day. And they were both trying to keep it that way.

"Kate, who's that comin' up the road?" Loren McKendrick squinted against the afternoon sunlight, shielding his eyes as he watched the approaching car slowly pull up in front of the house.

Kate joined him on the porch, a dishcloth in her hand.

They didn't know anyone who owned an electric-blue Coupe de Ville. She noted the Nevada tags on the front. No one came to mind.

A man got out and approached them. His black hair was peppered with gray, making him look very distinguished. There was something vaguely familiar about him, Kate thought. She'd never met him, and yet . . .

"Mr. McKendrick?" their visitor inquired, addressing Loren politely.

"Yep."

"I'm Amos Mallory. I was told in town that I could find Matt Farrell here."

"You were told right," Loren acknowledged. "He's down at the barn, working."

Kate handed the cloth to her father-in-law and started down the steps.

"I'll take you to him, Mr. Mallory," she said.

Farrell was surprised to see his visitor.

"What are you doing here, Amos?" he asked as he climbed down the ladder and dropped the hammer on one of the steps.

Amos looked relieved to see Farrell, Kate thought.

"I had to drive over to Sacramento and I thought I'd stop in on my way through town," Mallory replied.

Farrell laughed.

"Yeah, sure, Amos."

Kate was curious, but she left the two men to themselves. When Mallory left a little later she was still wondering what his relationship was to Farrell. Neither man had offered any explanations. They certainly played their cards close to the vest, she thought in annoyance. Mallory must be a gambler, too, she decided.

Vern Peterson, on his way to the ranch, had seen Mallory's car when the sheriff was only a short distance from the house.

"Everything okay, Kate?" Vern asked, leaning out his window a little.

"Everything's fine," she replied. "What brings you out here, Vern?"

"Just checking on you," he answered. The sheriff didn't look too happy. "I haven't found any record on Farrell, but when that stranger came asking about him, I thought I'd better make sure everything was all right out here."

Kate smiled and shook her head. The women at the Peterson ranch stayed inside. They cooked and sewed and had babies. The Peterson men took care of the ranching . . . and the protecting. Vern still had a hard time believing that the McKendrick women weren't like that.

"Thanks, Vern," she said. "Nice of you to think of us."

She didn't want to hurt his feelings, so she left it at that.

"Have you got any idea who might have beaten him up?" she asked curiously, not that she was really convinced that that was what had happened . . . but it was a possibility . . . and Kate tried to be fair-minded. After all, Farrell seemed to believe it.

Peterson snorted in derision.

"Nope. And I don't expect to," he said in disgust. He put the police car in reverse and waved good-bye. "See you, Kate."

Farrell, who'd been working not too far away, watched Kate go back inside. Now why would she ask a question like that? he wondered. Most townspeople put drifters and gamblers into a category of their own . . . people not to be believed . . . people not to be concerned about . . . maybe not even people at all . . . some kind of animal lowlife.

Kate was different. . . . He shook his head to clear it. He had to stop thinking about her like that. Just concentrate on your work, he told himself. If things went well, he'd be out of this backwater with the money he'd won from that jackass, Walker, in another week or so. . . . He could get back to his own life. . . .

On Saturday afternoon the minister dropped in.

To everyone's surprise, he brought Farrell's things.

After the two men had been introduced, Peter handed them over.

"Sorry they're in such bad condition, Matt," said the minister apologetically. "I happened across them when I was driving by the site for our new recreation hall. They were just scattered around in the dirt."

Farrell looked at his wallet. It was empty. That didn't come

42

as much of a surprise. His garment bag looked like it had been dragged through a dust storm, along with his clothing.

"Thanks, Vining."

"Don't mention it." Peter turned his attention to Kate. "Are you still planning on coming to the fund-raiser next weekend, Kate?"

She walked him back to his well-worn car.

"Yes. I wouldn't miss it!" she exclaimed.

"See you later, Kate."

As the minister drove off, Farrell joined her.

"What fund-raiser?" he asked.

"The church is holding a square dance next Saturday. Peter's trying to raise money to build a recreation hall so that the kids around here will have someplace to go for partying . . . the adults, too, for that matter. He's been holding different fund-raising events every couple of months. It looks like square dancing may be his best bet, if the money he made from the last one is any indication!"

"He gets a good turnout?" Farrell inquired with interest.

Kate looked at Farrell in surprise. It was the first interest he had shown in Still Waters's social life.

"Yes. Everybody around here has promised to go. If you want to see the people of Still Waters, the square dance next weekend is the place to be."

"You don't say," Farrell mused, resting a foot on the lowest bar of the fence next to them.

Kate looked at him, wondering if she should suggest what she was thinking. Why not? He had as much right as anyone to be there, she thought.

"You'd be more than welcome, if you'd like to go," she said. "Come with me if you like. A friend of mine is coming to pick me up. There'll be plenty of room in the truck."

Farrell looked at her in surprise.

"Aren't you afraid?" he asked.

She stared back. She was coming to recognize that impassive, steady-eyed expression of his. He wore it like a mask. It was a poker face if ever she'd seen one. She wondered what the man underneath it was really like. There was something about Matt Farrell that piqued her curiosity.

"Afraid?" she echoed. "Of you?"

43

He shrugged.

"You don't know me. For all you know I could be one of the most dangerous men in America," he said. "I'm not," he added. "But you have no way of knowing that."

"Farrell, I've lived out here almost my entire life. Most of the world is full of strangers, as far as I'm concerned. I judge a man by how he deals with me. You've worked hard, kept to yourself, been polite and entirely trustworthy from what I've seen." She grinned as her big black dog trotted across the corral to join them. "And I have my own law enforcement out here in case I'm misjudging you," she added with a nod in Doc's direction.

Farrell grinned back at her.

"That you do, ma'am," he acknowledged. "That you do."

CHAPTER THREE

"All you ladies chain to the left . . . stop at the fella you like the best . . . chain on back . . . now all join hands and circle right . . ."

The square dance was in full swing when Kate and Matt walked in. The caller was leading three squares of enthusiastic dancers through the patterns while the fiddlers sawed vigorously on their well-worn instruments.

"I better make sure those boys of mine don't get into the wrong punch!" Jerico blustered as she anxiously scanned the barn for her fast-disappearing offspring.

Jerico Johnson, unflappable owner of the General Store, warm-hearted mother-figure to half the town, long-time friend to Kate and the McKendrick clan, had only one Achilles' heel: her children. The rambunctious boys she was struggling to rein in were, as usual, giving her one heck of a run for her money. Kate was tempted to grin at the sight of Jerico's ample frame struggling to keep up with her much fleeter-of-foot kids. They'd leaped out of the truck like wild horses. Kate doubted that Jerico could corral them all in one place until the evening was half over!

Kate watched as the crowd swallowed Jerico. Now that she was alone with Farrell, she didn't quite know what to do with him. She hadn't intended this as a date, but she thought it would be rude just to walk off and leave him. After all, he didn't know anyone in Still Waters.

"Why don't you go on, Kate?" he said, as if sensing her unvoiced argument.

"And what will you do?" she asked, turning to look at him.

He didn't look too ill at ease, she thought. His clothes fit, even if they were a little mended here and there, but what could you expect of clothing that had been dumped in the street and stamped on? He was just lucky he'd recovered his things at all. At least he no longer had to wear borrowed clothes that didn't quite fit.

"I'll make out just fine," he replied. "I'm used to being an outsider, remember?"

He wasn't smiling, and there was something about his steady-eyed gaze that made her feel ambivalent about leaving him on his own. Kate didn't believe that he was as tough and uncaring as he tried to appear. That enigmatic facade he wore was becoming increasingly annoying to her. She kept wondering what the man underneath it was really like.

"Kate! So good to see you!" cried out Abigail Duncan as she rushed up to them with open arms. She was gingerly hugging Kate when she took a closer look at the man next to her. "And who is this handsome man you've brought with you, Kate McKendrick?" she cooed as she squinted curiously at Farrell.

Kate braced herself and replied.

"Abigail, this is Matt Farrell. Mr. Farrell, this is Abigail Duncan . . . our hostess."

Abigail's thin, colorless face froze and a small, strangled sound seemed to die in her throat.

"Wasn't it nice of the Duncans to offer the use of their barn for the fund-raiser?" Kate said sweetly as she disengaged herself from Abigail's rigid limbs.

Farrell tipped his head, but his eyes had a hard cast. He recognized the Mrs. Duncans of the world.

"It certainly was. Nice to make your acquaintance, ma'am," he said politely.

Mrs. Duncan tried to smile but only managed a grimace. She searched the room desperately for her husband, who had somehow been able to escape her.

"We were glad to be asked," Mrs. Duncan said, still looking flabbergasted. She craned her neck in the direction of the punch bowls. "I'd better see if I can locate Mr. Duncan," she murmured weakly. "If you'll excuse me . . ."

"How big is Mr. Duncan?" Farrell asked softly, bending toward Kate.

Kate gave him a perplexed look.

"Wally? Oh . . . maybe five feet five or so," she answered. "Why?"

Farrell gave her a twisted grin.

"Just wondering how big a guy was going to be sent to kick me out," he replied with a shrug.

"Don't be ridiculous!" Kate protested. Then she caught sight of sour-faced Abigail prodding her clearly unhappy husband in their direction.

Kate frowned. She sensed Farrell was moving away. Without looking at him she grabbed his elbow and started across the barn.

"Wally'll have to go through me first," she muttered angrily. "Honestly! Sometimes the people around here are enough to put your teeth on edge!"

Farrell was too surprised to resist. By the time Kate had pulled him into the crowd of people lining the far wall, it was too late to escape her grasp.

"Let me introduce you to a few people," she said confidently.

Farrell saw the hush settling across the cluster of people they were approaching. He'd seen closed looks like the ones on the faces staring at him many times in the past. He tried to free himself from Kate's grasp.

"Darlene, I'd like you to meet Matt Farrell," she said brightly.

Fifteen minutes later it was obvious even to Kate . . . the people of Still Waters were not about to open their arms to Matt Farrell.

"I'm sorry," she said, cheeks dark with embarrassment. "I really had no idea they'd all be so . . ."

"Bigoted?" Farrell asked.

Kate looked up at him, searching for how he really felt about it. It was hard to tell. That poker face of his sat on him like armor, she thought in frustration.

"So bigoted," she agreed. "I thought people around here could still find it in their hearts to be friendly to a stranger." She looked around at the dancers gathering to form new squares for the next songs. "Maybe they just need a little nudge in the right direction," she added.

Farrell saw the speculative gleam in her eye. He almost

47

frowned. What was she up to now? he wondered. With Kate he was constantly being surprised.

She grabbed his hand and turned toward him triumphantly.

"I've got it! They just need to warm up to you a little. If the other girls are second or third, nobody'll make much out of it. I'll break the ice for them! Come on, Farrell, let's dance!"

Farrell pulled back as she stepped toward the dance floor.

"Hey! Wait just one minute!" he protested. "I don't know anything about square dancing!"

"There's nothing to it. Just listen to the caller and watch what the other men do."

"But I don't want to dance!"

"Of course you do! And I'll be happy to be your first partner. You wanted to get to know something about the people of Still Waters, Farrell. Well, here's your foot in the door. Mingle a little after they've let their hair down! A man who'll square dance can't be all bad!"

When Kate got the bit in her teeth she was a hard woman to stop. Farrell found himself with three other couples in the middle of the barn a few seconds later.

"I hope you know what you're letting yourself in for, Mrs. McKendrick," he muttered.

She laughed softly, giving gracious smiles to the startled dancers.

"I'm not afraid of these people, Farrell," she said under her breath.

He looked down at her as the fiddlers struck up a tune.

"No. You certainly aren't."

The caller's singsong voice interrupted them.

"Bow to your partner . . . now bow to the corner . . . now bow to the couple across the road . . . and eight to the center then come on back . . ."

As they danced their way through the patterns Kate forgot why she'd dragged them onto the floor. Farrell hadn't been entirely accurate when he'd said he didn't know anything about square dancing, but what he didn't know he very quickly picked up. He was strong and gracious and light on his feet, she soon discovered. It wasn't just his reputation that attracted glances from the crowd after a couple of songs. It was Farrell the man.

Calico skirts and white ruffled petticoats swirled and flounced as men in Western-cut pants and shoestring ties strutted and laughed. The rhythmic country tunes, solid and simple, set a lively pace, but no one flagged. Each song was a little faster, the moves more intricate than the one before. By the time they'd been dancing for an hour, Kate and Farrell were both ready for a break.

"How about a visit to the punch bowl?" Kate suggested, fanning her face with her hand to cool off a little.

The crowd parted before them like the Red Sea. Farrell turned to Kate and frowned.

"Is this what you call 'letting their hair down' and 'warming up to a stranger'?" he inquired dubiously.

"Just keep your foot in the door, Farrell," Kate retorted testily as she silently swore at her unfriendly neighbors.

"Katie! Who *do* you have with you?" cooed a feminine voice just to their right.

Kate and Farrell turned their heads just in time to see Sissy Wells wiggle past a few men and join them at the punch table.

"Hi, Sissy," Kate replied, forcing herself to smile. She wasn't sure she was up to dealing with Sissy Wells tonight. "This is Matt Farrell," Kate said evenly. "Matt, this is Sissy Wells."

Sissy batted her eyes admiringly and held out her slender hand. Farrell automatically took it and shook hands. It seemed to Kate that it took an abnormally long time for them to let go of each other.

"Mr. Farrell," Sissy exclaimed, using the softest, silkiest voice Matt had heard in years. "You wouldn't by any chance be *the* Mr. Farrell?"

Kate stood by as a definite sense of annoyance grew in her. How could Sissy be so obvious? And why was Farrell accepting the attention with such . . . such . . . What did that look in his eyes mean, anyway, she wondered in exasperation!

"*The* Mr. Farrell?" he repeated questioningly, a hint of amusement lurking in his voice.

Sissy smiled coyly and stepped a little closer. Kate hadn't thought there was enough room for that, but somehow Sissy managed to keep a centimeter or two of space between her body and Farrell's.

"Why . . . the Mr. Farrell who cleaned everybody out at the card parlor not too long ago . . . then had"—Sissy's eyelids fluttered for a second—"some misfortune befall him on the way out of town."

Kate couldn't stand much more of this. They were staring into each other's eyes as if there were no one else in the room! What in the world was the matter with Farrell, anyway? Somehow she'd expected him to be more . . . more . . . More what? Kate tried to keep her expression reasonably cheerful, but the effort was beginning to get to her.

"I suppose I must be," Farrell acknowledged with a slight inclination of his head.

Sissy slipped her arm through Farrell's and smiled up at him, her face a portrait of rapt fascination.

"Why, gamblers are such exciting men, Mr. Farrell. *Do* tell me all about yourself. You can't *imagine* how boring it is to live in a little backwater town like Still Waters! I'm simply *dying* to hear all about the big world out beyond."

"Is that so?" asked Farrell in amusement. He glanced over petite Sissy's fluffy blond head and looked at Kate.

Before he could say anything, Kate lifted herself sufficiently from her state of amazement to smile graciously at them.

"Go right ahead," she told him, waving one hand for emphasis. Her eyes locked with Farrell's for a moment. She forced herself to shake off the strange feeling it gave her of being somehow connected to him. "Remember . . . this is a good chance to become acquainted with the people of Still Waters." Kate suddenly didn't want to let him go. She told herself that it was silly to feel that way. She forced herself to ignore it. "Go on. Sissy can help fill you in."

It was odd. It seemed to Kate that there was a flicker deep in Farrell's eyes. As if he was surprised at what she had said. Then it was gone. He nodded and turned his attention toward Sissy, who was tenaciously clinging to his side.

"Would you care for some punch, Miss Wells?" Farrell asked politely.

She giggled with pleasure.

"*Do* call me Sissy," she implored. "And may I call you Matt?"

"By all means."

Kate fought the urge to close her eyes in disgust at the too-saccharine tones. She picked her way through the people who'd gathered in front of the table and reached for a cup. One of Jerico Johnson's teenage sons saw Kate and tried to take off. Before he could make good his escape, Kate called out to him.

"Tad! Pour me a cup of punch, would you please?" Kate pleaded.

At the time Kate thought his face looked a little funny. For a moment she thought he was going to refuse outright. That was quite strange. Jerico's kids were a rambunctious lot, but they were well-mannered. His mother's training finally got the better of him. He filled the cup, mumbled something about having to go, and took off without a backward glance.

"Maybe it's me," Kate murmured to herself. "People seem happy to leave me tonight."

She took a sip of the punch. It was cool and sweet. She'd never tasted anything quite like it. She took another sip. It tasted even better.

"Evening, Kate," drawled a satisfied male voice just over her shoulder.

Kate whirled and found herself staring at T. J. Walker's throat. She looked up at him, unblinking.

"Hello, T.J. I'm surprised to see you here tonight."

"Why's that?"

T.J. always did rise to her bait, she thought as a smile played at her mouth.

"Because this is a charity event," Kate pointed out. When he merely looked at her blankly, she clarified it for him. "I always thought that Walker business interests were your only charities."

"Normally, I'd have to agree with you," T.J. replied with a shrug as he ran his eyes appreciatively over her slim figure. "But when I heard you were going to be here tonight, Kate, I made a special exception."

His voice had turned low and intimate and there was a strange light in his eyes. Kate hadn't felt so uncomfortable in his presence since they were teenagers. A long-forgotten memory teased her elusively.

Then she remembered.

He'd looked at her like that once before. It had been the night of a big dance in her freshman year in high school. He'd looked at her with that same calculating, speculative hunger. Kate remembered how unclean she'd felt . . . and how grateful she'd been to be in Seth's company for the evening.

Kate took a step back. She'd felt unclean then. And she felt unclean now. Funny how some things never seem to change, she thought. Only this time she was on her own. Seth wasn't here to help deflect T.J.'s unwanted attention.

This time, Kate, you have to handle it yourself, she told herself.

"Care to dance?" T.J. asked, holding out his elbow and bowing slightly. His eyes never left hers.

"No thanks, T.J.," she declined politely. "But don't let me stop you," she added, waving expressively toward the crowded barn. "I'm sure you can find a partner. The whole town's turned out, it seems."

Walker tucked her hand through his arm and held her firmly in place when she tried to pull away.

"Come on, Kate! Where's your sense of charity?" he challenged. "This is neutral territory. Let's put aside our disagreements for the evening. I can turn over a new leaf if you can."

Kate wasn't a fool. She didn't know what T.J. had in mind, but she was curious to find out why he was playing the gracious gentleman all of a sudden. He had to have something up his sleeve. Of that she was certain.

It took an effort, but she managed to smile at him in a halfway convincing manner.

"All right, T.J.," she declared. "You're on! A truce for the evening."

"Let's drink to that," he exclaimed, sounding more like his usual boisterous self. Before Kate could open her mouth to say no, T.J. had grabbed a cup of punch for himself and was refilling hers.

"To neighborliness," T.J. proposed, holding up his cup. Kate couldn't bring herself to refuse. That seemed so churlish. She raised up her cup. "To neighborliness," she repeated, watching him steadily over her punch. They lifted the cups and drank.

Kate fanned her throat with her hand.

"Does it seem hot in here to you?" she asked, beginning to feel really warm. It was odd, she thought. The barn wasn't heated, after all. It must be because of all these people. . . .

She was aware of his hand at her elbow steering her toward the barn door.

"Let's go out and cool off a little," he suggested. "You can tell me all about how that young sprout of yours is doing," he added blandly.

The caller sang out, ". . . then allemande left and promenade home . . ."

Matt was promenading the giggling bundle of blond energy when he caught sight of T.J. escorting Kate toward the door.

Sissy, who wasn't nearly as dumb as she looked, slyly assessed Matt's line of vision and took note of the departing twosome. Unlike Farrell, however, Sissy didn't bother to hide her reaction.

"Why that no-good, two-timing . . ."

The applause muffled the end of her sentence, but Farrell didn't need to hear it to know what she said.

He raised an eyebrow and looked down at her.

"T.J. a friend of yours?" he asked politely.

She stamped her tiny foot on the well-worn floorboards.

"Not anymore," she fumed, dragging Farrell along behind her as she headed for the punch bowls. "Tonight, Matt Farrell, *you* are my friend!" she declared emphatically.

Farrell knew in one swallow that the punch bowl wasn't going to help cool off the little firebrand next to him.

"Where are those boys?" cried Jerico as she pushed by him and ducked her head under the table in search of her thrill-seeking offspring. "When I get my hands on them! . . ."

"Lose some kids?" Farrell asked as his eyes crinkled with amusement.

Sissy was craning her neck to see if T.J. and Kate were returning, so Jerico was able to speak in private.

"Did you taste that stuff?" Jerico whispered, looking aghast as a blush darkened her ruddy cheeks.

"Packs quite a wallop," Farrell acknowledged with an affirmative nod of his head. "I didn't think they served stuff like this at country church socials," he added.

Jerico shook her head.

"They don't!" She leaned closer. "If Abigail Duncan finds out, she'll have a stroke and take the kids to court for sure!"

Farrell choked on his punch and put it down.

"That bad, huh?" he said in a strangled voice.

Jerico nodded her head and gave him a woebegone look.

"Worse. People are pretty straitlaced hereabouts, Farrell. The drinking and gambling are done in the places for them. Period." A thought suddenly occurred to her. "Say, didn't I see Kate over here?"

"Yes."

"Oh, no! Kate doesn't drink anything stronger than six-hour-old coffee! If she had a couple of cups of this, she won't know what hit her! It tastes just like some fruity syrup with soda water. She won't realize . . ." Jerico's eyes opened even wider as she noticed a woman nearby giggling between sips. "The tee-totaling women won't know it's got liquor in it, and the men'll be too sly to tell 'em. They'll just lap it up while the lappin's good." she wailed despairingly.

It was about then that Farrell realized how noisy it was becoming. People were talking very loudly and waving their hands a lot more than would be expected. And a lot of men were loosening their collars and looking pretty red in the face.

"What's in that stuff, anyway?" he asked in a conspiratorial whisper close to Jerico's ear.

"Lord only knows! I can't imagine what those boys could have gotten their hands on! But when I get my hands on them . . ."

A loud eruption of laughter across the room ended their conversation.

"Oh, no!" Jerico cried.

Abigail Duncan was being helped to a chair by one of the ladies as the men picked her husband, Wally, up off the floor.

"Must have had something that disagreed with 'im . . ." mumbled the man staggering past them on his way to the punch.

"Come on, Matt, honey. Let's go get a breath of fresh air!"

"See you later," Matt said to Jerico as Sissy hauled him in the direction of the door.

Normally, Farrell didn't let himself be pulled around this much. He was making a special exception tonight in general and now in particular. He was beginning to wonder if his fierce little boss was all right. Everything else seemed to be going into a noticeable decline.

Farrell had a rule about deteriorating situations like this. It was a very simple one: Leave before they have to carry you out. He stepped gingerly around an arguing couple and a glazed-eyed man swaying from one foot to the other.

"I think it must be about time to go," he murmured under his breath.

Kate didn't see them arrive. She was having trouble seeing at all. T.J. kept blurring in front of her. At times it almost looked like there were two of him. She was trying so hard to hear what he was saying, but it sounded as if he was mumbling from a long way away. She inhaled deeply and tried one more time.

". . . so I want you to know, Kate, anytime you'd like some help, I'd sure like it if you'd let me know," T.J. was saying. "It's the Major that's causing all the trouble between us . . . and I'm not going to stand by and watch without speakin' up anymore. . . . Did you hear me, Kate?"

He was peering down into her face with those beady little black eyes that reminded her of a rat's.

"The McKendricks are just fine," Kate replied, enunciating like an elocutionist. Thank God she could still talk, she thought.

T.J. grabbed her by the arms.

"It's not the McKendricks I'm offering to help," he said clearly. "You know that, Kate. Don't pretend that you don't!"

Kate wriggled her arms, but it just made the world spin.

He pushed her back against the barn as Sissy, who'd been standing in speechless rage, rediscovered her voice.

"And just *who* are you offering to help, T.J.?" she asked, her eyes narrowed into catlike slits.

T.J. was not pleased to see them.

"What are you doing out here, Sissy?" he asked coldly, including Farrell in the question by the nasty look he gave him.

Sissy wrapped herself a little closer to Farrell. Farrell saw the angry look in Walker's eyes change just a shade.

So, Sissy's your property, eh, Walker? Matt thought.

"Why, I'm dancing with my friend, Matt," she retorted, snuggling up against Farrell's arm and daring T.J. to do something about it.

Farrell couldn't see any advantage to being in the middle of a lovers' quarrel and tried discreetly to disengage himself.

"And I've been having a nice neighborly chat with my old friend T.J.," Kate said with exceptional clarity. She gazed up in fascination at T.J.'s confused expression. "Now, now, T.J. . . . I'm just trying to bury the hatchet."

T.J. opened his mouth to reply, but Kate beat him to it, unfortunately for her.

"But you know, ol' friend," she said, her speech beginning to slur just a little. "I still can't figure out why you'd be interested in helping me instead of siding with the Major?" She grabbed his Western jacket lapels with both hands and stood practically nose to nose with him. "Could you explain that, T.J.?"

Sissy shot out of her corner of the arena and yanked the speechless T.J. a foot away from Kate, who appeared totally shocked at the turn of events.

"Honey," Sissy said with sweet acid dripping from every vowel, "I'll tell you as soon as I hear the answer to that myself. Meanwhile, T.J. promised me a dance at this here hoedown, and I aim to claim it while the claiming's still good."

Kate nodded her head and waved a limp hand.

"Oh, sure, Sissy. Sor . . . Sorry about that . . . go right on . . ."

Sissy glared threateningly up at T.J., who was towering over her like an angry thundercloud. T.J. knew Sissy, however. Sissy was the type to take a stand when she was angry. And she was madder than hell right now. Not only would she make a scene, she'd have a knock-down, drag-out fight!

T.J. gritted his teeth and nodded at Kate. Then he held out his elbow to Sissy.

"That's right, honey," she said, her ice-hard eyes still staring daggers at him. "I'd carry on like you'd never forget." She snuggled up against him as they melted into the crowd. "But I'll make it up to you later . . . at my place, honey."

Farrell heard the music fade a little as the old barn door swung closed. When he looked back at Kate it was just in time to see her start to slide down the wall she'd been leaning on only a second earlier. He leapt forward and caught her under the arms. She looked up at him. He wasn't sure how much she really was seeing anymore. There was a helpless, open look in her soft green eyes that he'd never seen there before. It gave him a strange feeling somewhere in the region of his heart.

"Are you all right?" he asked doubtfully, propping her up against the wall.

"Sure," she replied, beginning to slide down again. "I'm jus' fine. . . ." Her head slumped forward against his chest and she went limp.

Farrell swore softly and lifted her up in his arms.

"I can see that!" he muttered sarcastically. He looked down at her gentle features, innocent and trusting in repose. "You are one stubborn woman, Kate McKendrick!"

It was cold outside. Farrell hugged her close, both to keep from dropping her and to keep them both a little warmer. He tried to think of something discreet to do with her. Somehow carrying her unconscious across the dance floor like this didn't sound like it would play too well in upright Still Waters! And they sure couldn't stand outside and freeze to death!

Jerico saved the day.

"Farrell? Is that you out there?" she hollered as she barreled outside, a small flock of teenage boys hanging their heads behind her. "We're goin' home!" Then she got close enough to see who was in his arms. "Oh, Lord!"

"She's all right," he said, giving her a reassuring grin. "Just a little too much fun, I guess."

Jerico started berating the boys all over again as they trooped toward her truck. She was still carrying on when Farrell carried Kate up the path at the McKendrick ranch.

"We'll be fine, Jerico," Farrell said as he urged her to go. "Keep your eyes on the road!" he added with a laugh. "Thanks for the ride."

Farrell struggled up the front-porch steps with Kate only to find the front door locked. He knocked softly, but got no reply. He stared at Kate's form in the darkness and tried to decide what to do. They couldn't stay out here, obviously. His eyes strayed down her figure. He could search her for a key, he thought reluctantly. She hadn't brought a purse. Damn! What in hell had happened to his luck? he wondered in frustration. And sitting at card tables didn't keep you in shape for heavy labor or carrying unconscious women, he realized as his arms began to ache.

He hoisted her over his shoulder and marched down the steps. Where in the hell was that damned unfriendly black dog of hers, anyway? he wondered irritably. Doc could have wakened the household with no problem!

Farrell carried her into the small cabin behind the barn where he'd been staying.

"Well . . . at least it's warm," he said as he kicked the door shut behind them and dropped Kate unceremoniously on the couch that folded out into a bed.

He shrugged off his own coat and dropped it on the far end of the sofa bed, then he turned his attention to removing Kate's.

He unfastened the front and slid one hand behind her back. In spite of his best intentions, the feel of her sank into his awareness. Her back was soft and firm, curving gently in all the right places. He swallowed and eased the coat off one soft shoulder. His hand lingered a little longer than absolutely necessary at each step in the process, in spite of the fact that he kept telling himself to hurry up and get this over with.

There was something exquisitely tantalizing about undressing her a little while she was in no position to notice it. He hung over her, resting his hands on the sofa, letting himself enjoy looking at her. The soft rise and fall of her breasts began to have a hypnotic effect on him, and he found himself wanting to touch her again. And not just to remove her coat, either.

He closed his eyes and swore silently.

Don't get mixed up with her, he told himself, as bitter memories began to plague him. It's just not in the cards. The deck was already stacked against him. She wasn't the type of woman to let herself get involved with a man like him, anyway.

Farrell took a deep breath and straightened up, turning his attention to the pot-bellied stove. He needed to find something else to do besides stare at her! He reached for the tin of coffee and gave the unconscious form on his sofa-bed a baleful glare.

He sincerely hoped that the smell of coffee would wake her up soon!

Eventually, it did, to his great relief.

"Mmmm . . ." mumbled Kate as she groggily opened her eyes and pushed herself up on one elbow. "What . . ."

She squinted her eyes and tried to focus. Farrell was floating on the old leather chair near the stove, his legs stretched out in front of him and crossed at the ankles, a cup of something cradled in his hands. Her head felt fuzzy and light. Her mouth tasted sweet and sticky . . . very odd indeed.

"I don't remember coming home," she said slowly, swinging her feet over the edge of the sofa and gripping the sides with both hands.

"You were a little under the weather," Farrell explained before draining his cup of coffee. "Like some coffee?"

"Please," she accepted gratefully. "What happened?"

Farrell poured her a cup of hot black liquid and walked across the small room to hand it to her.

"I'm afraid that punch you liked so much had aged a little."

Kate held her head with one hand and her coffee with the other.

"Aged?" she echoed dumbly. She took a swallow of the coffee. It jerked her upright. It also got her brain functioning. "You mean someone spiked it with alcohol?"

Farrell laughed.

"It tasted more like they'd spiked the alcohol with a little punch, if you ask me."

Kate managed a hazy smile.

"I never knew I had what it took to be a lush," she joked, giving a shaky laugh. She looked up at Farrell, who was still standing in front of her, looking down at her enigmatically. "You . . . carried me home?" she asked uncertainly.

He nodded.

"I tried to take you into the big house, but the door was locked and I wasn't sure how you'd feel about my waking the household under the circumstances," he explained. "I tried one knock, but no one answered. So I brought you here."

She was staring up at him with those wide-open eyes. Not quite as helpless-looking as before. But still . . . Farrell walked back to the stove and fiddled with it as a furrow appeared between his eyes. Damn but she was an attractive woman, he thought uncomfortably.

"I didn't want to wake up your little boy," he said awkwardly as he looked around the room.

The rough-hewn walls and handmade curtains of faded blue and white reminded him of the homes he'd never had and always envied as a child. He cleared his throat uncomfortably. He hated remembering that feeling.

Kate was still feeling wobbly, but she was perceptive enough to see Farrell was uncomfortable. Polite poker-faced Farrell was standing there like an awkward schoolboy! She blinked her eyes in surprise. He was apologizing for bringing her here and trying to explain why. . . .

"That was very considerate," she said quietly. "I'm sure both Pop and Jason would have been quite surprised. I've never had to be carried home before!" She laughed awkwardly. "And you're probably right . . . Pop would have understood eventually. Jason might have been more confused."

She sighed and added reluctantly, "And then he'd never let me forget it! Anytime Jason'd want to protest an order, he'd throw it back at me!"

Farrell grinned sympathetically.

"I imagine so, ma'am."

"Farrell . . . after all this, I think you might just as well call me Kate, don't you?"

He looked at her in silence.

"After all," she pointed out, "I hired you to work on the ranch in return for room and board. . . . Nobody said you'd have to carry the boss home!"

He laughed shortly and shrugged.

"Whatever you say," he agreed.

Kate stood up. The world seemed to move a little. She sat down.

"Just sit there till things stop spinning," he suggested.

"I'm afraid I'll have to take you up on that," she acknowledged apologetically.

They sat in awkward silence. Only the crackle of the fire in the old stove could be heard. Finally, Kate couldn't stand it anymore.

"You know, Farrell, I still hardly know anything about you. You've been a great hired hand, but . . . tell me . . . how'd you get into gambling?" she asked curiously.

"I was good at it. It was a way to make a living."

Kate gave him a narrow-eyed look.

"But how in the world did you get started? Were your folks gamblers?"

Kate saw the slight stiffening of his back. She was learning to watch him more closely than most people she knew. She had to if she wanted to read him. When she saw that reaction she felt a small feeling of triumph. She'd see what was hidden behind that cool facade if it took every trick she could think of! For some reason, it was important. Kate couldn't remember ever being so curious about a person in her entire life. But then she'd never met a man like Matt Farrell before. . . .

"In a way, I suppose they were," he replied. "I never knew my father." That wasn't precisely the case, but it was close enough, he thought.

"Your mother raised you alone?" Kate asked curiously.

She kept her voice neutral. She had the feeling that Farrell would clam up if she showed much sympathy. He was the kind of man who'd take a woman's expression of sympathy as a form of pity. And he wasn't the type to welcome pity.

"Yeah."

"No brothers or sisters?"

"Nope."

"Around here that can be a tough life for a woman," she observed.

Bull's-eye. Kate's shrewd arrow hit the mark. An expression of sympathy for his mother was quite another thing entirely. . . .

Farrell ran his hand over the worn clean curtain.

"Yes. She had it tough all right. She worked in the fields as a migrant worker . . . worked cleaning toilets in backwater motels . . . a ranch cook during roundups . . . a maid for people who made a point of paying as little cash as possible for her twelve-hour days, forget health benefits or social security!" he said, the bitterness coming through to Kate's attentive ear. "She'd have loved a house like this," he remarked. "It feels like a home should . . . warm and lived in . . . full of memories . . . full of the past and with hope for the future. . . ."

Farrell suddenly realized how much he'd let spill out and shut his mouth. His hand dropped to his side. He shoved his fists into his pockets and stared at Kate. Why had he told her that, anyway? It was dangerous to tell people things, he reminded himself. They get to know you that way. Then they use you . . . or can use your weaknesses against you. . . .

Kate watched him close up on her and a sense of loss came over her. The man underneath was tantalizing. She wished he'd

61

stayed a little while longer. She wouldn't rush it, though. Maybe next time he'd trust her a little more. . . .

"Is she still living?" Kate asked cautiously. She wasn't sure. Farrell had been speaking in the past tense . . . and he'd seemed . . . sad.

He nodded.

"Yeah. Lives down in Fresno."

That was obviously all he cared to share. Kate let it go at that.

She looked at her watch and her mouth fell open in surprise.

"I'd better get a move on," she said with firm conviction.

She made an effort to stifle the dizziness as she stood up. Farrell crossed the room and helped her on with her coat. Dizzy or not, it was long past the time she should have gone, he thought uncomfortably.

He helped her walk back to the big house, keeping a hand under her elbow and a polite distance between them. He watched her fish a key out from behind the porch swing where it hung on a small rusty hook.

She practically tripped over Doc on the way in.

Farrell looked down at the dog.

"Man's best friend!" he muttered disbelievingly.

Kate gave him a questioning look.

"He slept through my discreet knock. I figured at least he'd wake your father-in-law."

Kate ruffled Doc's black fur as the dog stared suspiciously at Farrell.

"Doc doesn't bark," she explained. "He just bites. He was probably lying in wait behind the door just hoping you'd try to come in," she laughed. "Isn't that right, Doc?"

The two inscrutable males studied each other. The two-legged one tipped his head respectfully at the mistress of the house and backed out the door.

"Night, ma'am."

"Kate," she corrected him in a no-nonsense voice.

"Kate," he amended.

She closed the door and watched his tall masculine figure

disappear in the darkness as he walked back to the old homestead behind the barn.

His rough voice stayed with her, though.

Kate's last conscious memory was the sound of her name as Farrell had said it . . . Kate. . . .

CHAPTER FOUR

Sunday morning Kate found out what it felt like to be hung over . . . a feeling she dearly hoped never to experience again. While she cringed at every scrape of a shoe on the church floor, the Johnson boys hung their heads and listened to the Reverend Mr. Vining expound on the virtue of forgiveness. The nasty looks they got from their neighbors as they were leaving didn't encourage them to believe the congregation would be practicing what Mr. Vining was preaching in the near future, however.

Loren McKendrick gave Kate and Matt each a peculiar, scrutinizing look the morning after the square dance, but whatever he was thinking he kept to himself. Farrell was surprised at that. Surprised and unexpectedly pleased. No one had ever passed up a chance to grill him on a suspected infraction of community morals or mores.

Farrell felt a sense of gratitude for McKendrick's silence. For once he was being treated like an equal . . . like someone deserving of the same level of respect anyone should have.

The McKendricks had no idea that's how it seemed to Farrell. They treated everyone as fairly as they could . . . unless they had good reason not to.

Farrell was stretched out in the barn, pitching nails into an old tin cup, when the pint-sized whirlwind blew through the doors.

"Hi, Mr. Farrell!" Jason shouted cheerily as he slowed to a halt at the gambler's side. "What're you doin'?"

"Pitching nails."

"Can I pitch nails too?" Jason asked hopefully, his bright eyes vacillating between Farrell's face and the nearby can of nails.

Farrell smiled.

"Sure, kid. Help yourself."

"Oh, boy!" Jason crowed in delight as he scooped up a fistful. "What're you s'pose to do?"

Farrell showed him.

"Do you know any other games, Mr. Farrell?" Jason asked a little while later, when pitching nails had lost some appeal.

Farrell looked at the earnest, curious little face and nodded his head. He couldn't remember the last time he'd played with a child. Even when he was a kid himself, he hardly remembered playing. He ruffled Jason's curly blond hair and was rewarded with a shy, dimpled grin.

"Sure, kid . . . but don't you have some chores to do this afternoon?"

"Naw. Mom says Sunday's the day of rest and at least some-one in the family should be ob . . . observing it." Jason strug-gled manfully over the long word and giggled when he realized he'd gotten it out. "Playing's my favorite way to rest!"

"Mine too," Farrell laughed. "You like card tricks, Jason?"

"Oh, yes!" Jason shouted enthusiastically, then added, less confidently, "What's a card trick?"

Farrell pulled an old deck of cards out of his pocket and began to shuffle it.

"Well . . . how about if I show you . . ."

An hour later Jason was still begging for more. Farrell skill-fully shuffled the deck. Cards snapped softly as he deftly manipulated them and stacked them, pulling jacks and queens from behind Jason's ear . . . making an ace of hearts turn magically into an ace of spades . . . making a card disappear from the deck, then miraculously making it reappear once more.

Jason looked up soulfully at the man of few words next to him.

"Could I do that?" he asked wistfully. "Could you show me, Mr. Farrell?"

"Well . . ." Farrell looked doubtful. Jason's face fell. Farrell felt his heart melt. "There's no harm in trying, I guess."

"I'm glad you came to work for us," Jason said, bursting with plans for the future. "You can teach me lots of tricks, and we can play on Sundays like this . . . right here in the barn."

"That's nice of you to feel that way," Farrell said uneasily.

"You won't have to go away, will you?" the little boy asked. He recalled his mother saying something about how long Farrell would be staying, but he couldn't quite remember what it was.

Farrell didn't know what to say. He'd seen everything he'd ever been attached to cut out of his life at one time or another as a child. He still had vivid memories of those unhappy times. He didn't want Jason to be hurt like he had been . . . not that his leaving could mean that much, of course, he hastened to remind himself.

"Do you have a home someplace?" Jason asked curiously.

That was a good question. Farrell had never really thought about it. He thought of his apartment in Reno. He certainly didn't think of it as a home. It was a place to sleep, shower, and dress. Period. It warehoused a few possessions that meant very little to him.

"No. Not really."

Jason struggled to imagine how anyone could exist without a home. Adults were different, he knew. But surely everyone had a home to go to. . . . He chewed on his tongue with a serious expression on his puzzled little face.

"But you have a mom and dad, don't you?"

Farrell fanned the cards out on the old oak floor.

"I've got a mom, but she lives alone." He gave Jason a level, man-to-man look. "When I grew up I had to get out on my own. I couldn't keep leaning on my mother."

Jason stared at Farrell with big eyes and open mouth. The idea of moving away from home had obviously never crossed his little mind.

"Oh." Then he returned to the other part of his question. "What about your dad?"

"My mom raised me alone. I didn't know my dad."

"Me neither."

Farrell was tempted to ask about Jason's father, but he was afraid he might stir up unhappy memories for the boy. Jason, however, gave him what he wanted anyway.

"My daddy's name was Seth McKendrick and he loved me a lot. He died when I was a baby." Jason's face clouded. "I wish he hadn't died. I wish he was here and could play with me . . . and . . . and teach me card tricks and things. . . ."

The door to the barn creaked as Kate opened it.

"Jason! There you are!"

Kate saw the wistful, longing look on his little face. He was looking up at Matt Farrell like a lonesome puppy. And Farrell was sitting there looking for all the world like a man staring at a ghost from his past.

"Mr. Farrell was showing me some tricks, Mommy!" Jason exclaimed as he scrambled to his feet. "And guess what! He doesn't have a daddy, just like me . . . and he doesn't have a home to go to . . . so can he stay here?"

Jason was an expert at constructing run-on sentences. No one ever got a word in until he'd gotten to the end of it. As usual, the adults were struggling with all the conclusions he'd already jumped to and trying to figure out how to refute his logic without taking up the rest of the afternoon in a complicated explanation.

Kate tried first.

"Mr. Farrell has a home, Jason. Everyone has a home to go to."

"But he *said* he didn't, Mommy!"

"He's just staying here until he can make plans, Jason. We can't pay him, and everyone needs a paying job," Kate reminded him patiently.

Still, Kate wondered what had started all this . . . and why Farrell had said he didn't have a home. . . . Of course, he *was* a gambler, she told herself. Maybe gamblers didn't have homes for all she knew.

Jason's chin stuck out defiantly.

"But he doesn't have anywhere to go if he doesn't have a home so we should let him stay here just like we let Doc stay here when he didn't have a home to go to."

Kate looked at her strong-willed little boy in exasperation.

"Doc's a dog, for heaven's sake, Jason! That has nothing to do with Mr. Farrell!"

"It's not fair!" Jason protested loudly. He gave Farrell a worried look. "But you'll stay, won't you?" he asked anxiously.

Farrell looked from Jason to Kate. He wasn't sure what he should say.

"Mr. Farrell has his own life to lead, Jason," Kate said as gently and as firmly as she could. Her eyes went from her disappointed son to the hard-to-read man next to him. "He's welcome to stay on if he likes, but we can't make him stay, Jason. We don't have much to offer."

Farrell knew she meant it. Kate, like her dog, didn't bluff or offer false promises. And at that moment he realized that what she had to offer was worth more than gold. She just had no way of knowing how a man like him would feel about it, he reflected.

Farrell thought about the money Amos had brought him. It had been sitting in his wallet for over a week. He'd been here long enough to size up the Walkers and the card playing. Why was he still hanging around, then? He looked at Kate McKendrick's straight, slim figure . . . light brown hair, braided in one long rope hung down her back. . . . The cool fall air still clung to her heavy coat. . . . It mingled with the smell of fresh wood and straw in the old barn. He remembered the home-cooked meals and simple camaraderie as they all pitched in to do the work around the ranch.

That was why he'd stayed. It felt like a home.

"I haven't finished the job here yet," Farrell remarked slowly. "I like to finish what I start."

Kate cocked her head to one side. That sounded like an excuse if ever she'd heard one. Yet she wasn't about to point that out. She was grateful that he was willing to stay a little longer. She was growing used to having him around. She'd miss him when he left, she realized, a little surprised at that.

"We'd be indebted to you," was all she said.

They looked at each other in silence.

"Dinner'll be ready soon," she said briskly. "Why don't you come up to the house and get washed up?"

"Can Mr. Farrell show me more tricks after dinner, Mom?" Jason asked with fervent hope written all over him.

"Mr. Farrell may want to take it easy," Kate said diplomatically as she held the barn door for the little dynamo.

Farrell pulled on his jacket and braced the door for her. They stood a foot apart when he looked down at her with smiling eyes.

"That's how I take it easy, ma'am," he interjected.

Kate was awash in unexpected warmth as his gaze bore into her. His voice had had the oddest effect. Like hot chocolate on a cold day, it warmed her heart. It made her want to reach out and touch him, to feel her palm against the hard plane of his cheek . . . To see his veiled eyes revealed a little more as they really were . . . To know him . . . really know him.

She felt the yearning in her soul and tried to tell herself that she was just a little lonely. It wasn't anything to pay attention to, not really. She caught her lower lip between her teeth and ducked out of the barn, not daring to say more. She hoped it would look like she was simply in a hurry to catch up with Jason.

She didn't fool Matt, however. He'd felt it too. It takes one to know one, he thought as he followed them up the rise to the big house. Even though she was bundled up in heavy clothes, he enjoyed watching Kate's no-nonsense yet feminine gait.

Everyone enjoyed dinner that night. They talked only a little. They enjoyed the silences like friends accustomed to them. Jason held court and the three adults indulgently played audience for him until it was time to clear away the plates. Matt helped Kate with the dishes, and Loren herded a protesting Jason into the bathroom for his bath.

The evening ended as most of them had recently. Jason fell asleep on Kate's lap in the middle of a story while Loren and Farrell sparred in a friendly game of checkers.

When Farrell got up to leave a little later, Kate gave him an extra comforter.

"It's turning colder every night," she explained as she gave him the handmade quilt.

Their hands brushed each other's arms, and they stood awkwardly in the doorway looking at one another in the shadows.

"Thank you," Farrell said, clearing his throat. "Good night."

"Good night, Farrell."

Holding back the starched white lace curtain, she watched him walk through the darkness. She was becoming dangerously accustomed to him, she realized. Even watching his easy stride was a small pleasure she would miss when he left. She lowered her eyes for a moment. The touch of his hand was still as real as it had been just minutes earlier.

She raised her eyes in time to see Farrell disappear into the darkness behind the barn.

Kate didn't know what she wanted, and for once, she was a

little afraid to find out. Her life had been difficult before he came, but in a way it had been simple and uncomplicated in spite of the problems. She had always felt that she could handle the challenges of being a rancher. She'd never doubted she could win.

She wasn't so confident where Farrell was concerned.

She stood in stunned silence as she finally admitted the real problem. Farrell made her feel like a woman again. It opened her up to a whole set of challenges she wasn't at all sure she could control. She stared blankly into the darkness.

The worst part was, she loved the way he made her feel. She loved it. And if he'd stayed instead of gone . . . She closed her eyes and saw him coming closer. She imagined that he brushed his lips across her cheek, that his hand caressed her breast and . . .

She bit her lip and blinked her eyes. What was she doing? Dear heavens, what *was* she doing? she asked herself in desperation.

Loren studied her curiously. He went up the stairs to his room without saying what was in his mind. Sometimes it was better to keep your opinions under your hat, he advised himself. Kate was a big girl. And she had a sound head on her shoulders. He'd trust her judgment as far as Farrell was concerned. From what he'd seen of Farrell in the past couple of weeks . . . that didn't look to be much of a risk.

As far as Loren McKendrick was concerned, Matt Farrell looked all right. And if it turned out that they were both wrong about Farrell . . . well, he'd just have to deal with that when the time came.

"We need more nails," Farrell observed as he climbed down the ladder in mid-week. He surveyed the nearly completed wall that divided the barn in half. "What's this going to be when it's finished, anyway?"

Kate latched the half door on Calamity's stall and joined him.

"That's my ace in the hole, I hope," she said.

Farrell grinned slightly.

"I didn't know you were a gambling woman, Kate," he teased.

70

Kate put her hands on her jean-clad hips and looked up at him saucily.

"Every woman worth her salt's a gambler, Farrell. Didn't you figure that out yet?"

"I can't say that I'd ever noticed that," he replied, looking decidedly unconvinced. He laid down the hammer and crooked an elbow through one of the ladder's rungs. "All the women I've met seem just the opposite, as a matter of fact."

Kate shook her head.

"Then you've been keeping pretty poor company, if you ask me, Farrell!" she remarked tartly.

Farrell acknowledged the jibe with a quirk of his brow.

"Why do you think women are gamblers at heart?" he asked curiously. It was a pretty bizarre idea to his way of thinking.

"Why, because life's just one gamble after another," she argued. "Whether to finish school or drop out . . . whether to go out with this guy or the other one . . . whether to get married . . . taking the chance on having kids and raising a family . . . Why, Farrell, I can't think of a single thing that isn't a gamble when you get right down to it!"

The unheated air had chilled her skin. Farrell looked at her in fascination, drinking in the sight of peach-colored cheeks and clear, fresh skin, clean-scrubbed and sparkling like newly polished china. Kate was the picture of healthy, wholesome living . . . a pretty country girl with fire and sparkle that bubbled up from wellsprings of inner strength and conviction.

He realized he was staring and started looking around for something else to focus on. It didn't help, though. He felt the steady thud of his heart and knew she was under his skin in a very special way.

Farrell pulled on his coat.

"So what, exactly, is your ace in the hole . . . if you don't mind my asking, of course."

Kate watched his fingers push the buttons through the holes of his coat. She was struck once again by the sensitive lines. He had strong, lean fingers. She shoved her hands into her pockets and walked stiffly toward the door. Each step of the way she tried to shake off the feeling that had been gradually overtaking her ever since he'd come to the ranch. She couldn't do it. Each day it simply became a little worse. It was a weak, trembling kind of sensation . . . and at the same time it wasn't. . . . It was glorious and wild and a little overwhelming.

Cut it out, Kate, she reprimanded herself sternly. Cut it out.

"I'm going into business with my sister next summer, if everything works out," Kate explained in a distant voice. "We're going to use this as a work and display area for some of the handicrafters around the Sierra Nevada. I'm going to take in a few boarders next year too . . . sort of like a dude ranch, I guess you could say. Between that and the craft center, I'm hoping to make enough extra money to get the cash flow back into the black around here."

A blast of chill air hit them as they stepped outside.

"I'll get Pop and Jason," Kate said as she hurried away.

"I'll get the wagon," Farrell said.

It had become a comfortable habit between them, going into town for supplies. Now that it was cold, Kate was trying to stock up for the winter. They were bringing back more staples and feed than the two of them could carry. It had come as a shock to Farrell the first time Kate had hitched Calamity to an old, single-harness buckboard.

"Saves on gas," Kate had explained curtly as she'd fastened the leather harness. "Besides, I had to sell the truck last winter for cash to pay Pop's doctor bills." She'd grinned mischievously. "Lucky that Still Waters still has its hitching posts, huh?"

Farrell had taken over hitching up Calamity without comment.

By the time Kate had corralled her family and herded them down to the buckboard, man and beast were ready and waiting.

There were dark-gray winter storm clouds gathering overhead as they pulled up in front of the General Store. As it turned out, there were storm clouds inside as well.

"Jason, go help Grandpa to the doctor's office," Kate ordered her fidgeting son as she gave him a hug good-bye. "And you mind, d'you hear?"

"Yes, Mommy," Jason acquiesced, his little chest practically sticking out with pride at his responsibility. "Come on, Grandpa," he shouted.

"I'm not hard of hearin', Jason," Loren grumbled as he limped along behind his cheerful escort.

The moment Farrell stepped into the store he knew they were going to have trouble. T.J. and some of the Walker ranch hands were there, and they were strutting like they owned the place.

"Kate. Farrell," T.J. grunted, acknowledging their arrival with a brief nod of his head.

"Afternoon, T.J.," Kate replied coolly as she walked by on her way to the sacks of feed grains piled at the back of the old building.

Jerico was nowhere in sight. Only Tad and two of his brothers were there. One of the Walker hands bought some loose tobacco and cigarette papers, plunking down his money by the register and giving Farrell a speculative look while he waited for his change.

"How's the work comin' along, Kate?" T.J. drawled, casually draping an arm over the pile of feed sacks next to her.

Kate looked over the prices. She answered without bothering to look at Walker.

"Just fine, T.J. Did you want to come out and help?"

T.J. laughed and shook his head.

"Sure, Kate. But I'd like something besides money for my effort."

"Is that so?" she asked, not terribly interested. As far as she was concerned, talking with T.J. was one of life's great wastes of time. You never got anywhere with him. T.J. was interested only in T.J. He didn't know the meaning of the word "compromise."

"Sure," he said in what she supposed he meant as a sexy voice. "I'd come out there this afternoon if you'd just agree to go to dinner with me Friday night."

"No thanks, T.J.," Kate said dryly. "But tell me," she asked, looking at him curiously, "why the sudden change of heart? First at the dance . . . now here."

He threw up his hands as if in surrender and gave her his most innocent, wide-eyed look.

"I told you, Kate. Your problems are the Major's doing. I thought he'd have let up before now." He gave her a warm look and leaned toward her. "You know I've always been soft on you, Katie."

"You could have fooled me," she muttered with a forced, insincere smile. "Don't worry, T.J., I'll manage." Then a thought occurred to her. "But you wouldn't care to tell me just why the Major is dead set on getting my land, would you?" she asked challengingly.

T.J.'s eyes turned blank and he shrugged.

"Just partial to it, I reckon. It's pretty good grazing land," he replied vaguely. "Some of it could be annexed to expand the town limits some."

Kate nodded her head and turned back to her selection of feed. She'd managed to get some for the cattle by way of an old friend of her brother-in-law across the valley, but poor Calamity's supply was about gone. They were overdue for the first snowfall and Kate wanted everything ready for winter before it came.

"Tad, I'd like three of these," she said, indicating the stack next to her. "Farrell can carry it out."

Tad nodded nervously and rang it up as Farrell hoisted the first sack onto his shoulder and exited the store. As Kate collected the rest of her purchases Tad dutifully totaled them, nervously glancing at the cowboys lounging around the old store.

"Thanks," Kate said as she paid.

"Sure, Miz McKendrick," Tad responded.

"Say, Tad," T.J. drawled, "I could use a little help out back with that order we're pickin' up today."

"Sure thing, Mr. Walker." Tad hurried around the counter and followed T.J., who was striding easily out the back door.

"And bring that brother of yours," T.J. ordered.

Tad frowned as he saw who was being left in the store. He had a bad feeling about this. But T.J. was repeating his order. And this time he didn't sound too happy at having to say it.

"Come on, Deke," Tad muttered. "Maybe with the both of us it won't take so long."

Deke pulled off his long apron and followed Tad outside. One of the ranch hands closed the door after them, then turned and leaned his back against it.

Farrell was bending down to pick up the last sack when Sissy Wells bounced into the store.

"Kate! I've been looking for you to come into town all week! I can't believe I've finally found you!"

Kate's mouth nearly fell open in surprise. She and Sissy had never been close friends. Their paths rarely crossed at all over the years, in spite of the fact that Still Waters was a small town.

"I *really* need your advice," Sissy gushed, her eyes wide open and pleading. "Could you please step next door for just a second, honey? I promise, it won't take much time at all."

"What exactly do you need help with, Sissy?" Kate asked, unable to imagine what it could possibly be.

Sissy looked coquettishly at the Walker ranch hands and lowered her voice to a whisper.

"It's . . . private, Katie. Please . . . just a few seconds of your time . . . I don't want to discuss it in front of the men."

That really got Kate's curiosity. A girl-to-girl talk with Still Waters's resident woman-of-doubtful-moral-character? Kate gave Farrell an apologetic look.

He'd been standing in silence, with the last sack slung over his shoulder.

"I'll be right back, Farrell." He'd be all right, she told herself. After all, all he had to do was carry the last bag of feed outside and put it on the buckboard.

He nodded and began crossing the store as the door shut behind the departing women. The bell hadn't stopped jangling when he felt a hand on his shoulder.

"Not so fast there," growled the owner of the hand as his fingers closed painfully over Farrell's collarbone. "We have a message for you, gamblin' man."

The store was suddenly deadly quiet. Out of the corner of one eye Farrell could see one of the other men pulling the shade partway down the front door and turning to lean against it. The two remaining men began moving toward him like slow, circling wolves planning to close in for the kill.

"What message is that?" Farrell asked evenly as he sized up the opposition.

"You've overstayed your welcome. It's time for you to be movin' on."

There was something familiar about the voice. Farrell had a good memory for people. And for everything about them. This man's voice . . . and his aura of cheap violence . . . and the crude grip . . .

"Is that so?" Farrell said in surprise. "Why, everybody's made me feel so welcome!" he exclaimed in mock surprise.

"Like you gents, for example. Why, I've never met a more enthusiastic welcoming committee!"

"Yeah?" sneered the tall, weather-beaten man coming toward him. "Well, you ain't seen nothin' till you've seen our good-bye party!"

"I expect this is it," Farrell muttered cynically, tensing his muscles for fight.

"You expect right," snarled the man behind him.

Just as the man in front of him began to take a swing at him, Farrell dumped the sack of grain back onto the man behind him and stepped smartly to one side saying, "Here, hold this, would you, pal?"

The recipient of the heavy sack grunted and staggered under the unexpected weight just as his sidekick's fist connected with his jaw, flooring him.

The tall cowboy was temporarily stunned into gaping at his fallen buddy.

"Damn, Crowley! Sorry 'bout that."

Crowley was swearing angrily and trying to get up off the floor while rubbing his painful jaw.

"Watch who you're hittin', Roebuck!"

Meanwhile, Farrell had backed around to the far edge of the store with the third man still stalking him.

"Tell me," Farrell said, never letting his eyes leave his pursuer's. "How much is Walker paying you for this little farewell?"

"If you think I'm dumb enough to answer that, Farrell, you'd better think again."

"You take the left, Grady," Crowley snarled. "Roebuck, you take the right." He grinned nastily. "And I'll go up the center."

Farrell was backed against the wall, a ring of checker tables and chairs between him and his attackers. No one suspected what was going on inside the Johnson store. The town was deserted, even by Still Waters's standards.

Well, at least this time I'm not doped up and half drunk, Farrell thought. When the first punch came he was ready.

"That was why you brought me over here?" Kate exclaimed as she stood in the middle of the beauty parlor and stared at the picture Sissy was holding up.

Sissy frowned petulantly.

76

"Well, what's wrong with that, Kate?" she asked peevishly. "I thought you might give me an opinion, that's all. I mean . . . it's a big decision, you know . . . whether to change my hair color to red." She grabbed a fluffy red wig from a nearby mannequin and stuffed her head into it. "I'd look like this. . . . Do you think it's pretty, Kate?"

Kate pressed her lips together in annoyance. She could not remember Sissy Wells ever asking any woman's opinion on her hairstyles or makeup. Sissy liked to walk to the beat of her own cosmetic drummer. All you had to do was look at her wild, sensuous selections to figure that out! This whole thing felt very contrived to Kate.

"Why did you really bring me over here, Sissy?" Kate asked crossly.

Jason was pulling his grandfather along the wooden plank sidewalk that ran from the doctor's office to the General Store.

"Come on, Grandpa," he whined in a pleading little voice. "I forgot to tell Mom to get some licorice sticks . . . and she'll probably leave and then I won't have any. . . . Come on! Before she gets in the buckboard! Please, Grandpa!"

Loren hobbled along as fast as he could, grateful for his cane every step of the way.

"All right, Jason! There's no hurry, though. If she's finished I'll get you some licorice before we leave town."

Poor Jason was so anxious to get his little hands on the coveted sweet that he didn't hear his grandfather's reassuring words. He just kept pulling like the little-engine-who-could.

"Hey!" cried Jason as he dropped to a halt in front of the entrance. "It's closed!" he wailed in deep disappointment.

Loren stared at the pulled shade, perplexed. There was no sight of anyone in their wagon hitched in front. Door closed and shade pulled in the middle of the day? He scratched his head.

Then they heard the muffled sound of furniture crashing.

Loren shoved the little boy in the direction of the sheriff's office.

"Go get the sheriff, Jason!"

He tried the door. It didn't budge. Kate joined him, running as she saw him put his shoulder into the door. Sissy Wells was calling after her about something. Before Kate could ask what was going on, they heard another loud crash and the grunt of men fighting.

Kate and Loren heaved themselves in unison against the door. It gave way, with Loren hanging on to the doorknob to keep from falling face forward into the store. Kate, not having anything to hang on to, blasted into the stand of ropes and lariats coiled just inside. As she quickly plucked herself out of the tangles, the cowhand who'd been leaning against the door reached for Loren.

"Oh, no you don't!" Kate muttered angrily. She grabbed a heavy coil of rope and whacked the man over the head with it.

He sank blissfully into unconsciousness at her feet.

"You always were handy with a rope," her father-in-law noted admiringly as he stepped over the body.

One of the other cowboys had just been shoved backward toward them. McKendrick held out his cane and caught the man just behind the heel of his boot, sending the disreputable-looking cowpoke crashing helplessly onto his back. Unfortunately for him, he struck his head on a stack of metal buckets on the way down. The would-be assailant gave them one, last stunned look before his eyes gently closed and he joined his sidekick in slumberland.

Kate grinned at her satisfied father-in-law.

"You're doing pretty good in the cane-tackling contest, Pop."

The sound of a body crashing into a pile of canned goods jerked their attention over to the far corner where Farrell was still scuffling with two men.

One was trying to pick himself up from the tumble of cans while the other landed a hard right into Farrell's jaw. Kate winced and leaped forward. Farrell ducked the next punch and came up jabbing at his adversary's midsection. Kate heard the breath whoosh out.

"Not bad, Farrell!" she hooted. "All that ranch work seems to have brought out your best."

Farrell, breathing hard and bleeding from a cut at the corner of his mouth, frowned as his fist connected with the jaw of the man in front of him. The man fell to the floor unconscious.

The man who'd finally extracted himself from the cans was

leaping toward Farrell, who stepped aside and broke a chair over his attacker's back, sending him out of the fight as well.

The lone remaining adversary, who was guarding the back door, abandoned his post and dove toward Farrell's back. Kate, however, had seen him and moved faster. She caught him in midair with the coil of rope in her hand, sending him sprawling, headfirst, into some horse blankets piled behind the cracker barrel.

Farrell whirled just in time to see the cowboy land and go limp. He wiped the back of his hand across his bleeding mouth and looked up at Kate.

"Thanks."

"You're welcome," she replied.

Kate looked him over. His clothing was rumpled and his shirttail had been pulled loose. There was a bruise beginning to swell on his cheek, and from the way he was gingerly touching his ribs, she guessed that he'd taken a couple of hard blows there, too.

She didn't know whether she felt more furious at his attackers or anguished at his being hurt. The two emotions raged within her, leaving her momentarily speechless.

She bent over and plucked his coat from the floor as he tucked in his shirt and ran his hands through his hair. By the time she handed it to him, empathy had won out over anger.

"Are you all right?" she asked, trying not to sound as concerned as she really was.

Farrell's grin looked more like a grimace of exasperation.

"Yeah," he said, shrugging it off as if it happened to him all the time.

"What started it, anyway?" she asked pointedly.

Farrell took the coat from her and put it on.

"Damned if I know. People around here just don't seem to enjoy my company."

Kate frowned as she thought about Sissy's sudden interest in feminine advice and T.J.'s timely removal of Tad and Deke. Before she could voice her thoughts, there was a thunder of feet through the front door.

"Gee, Mom! What happened?" cried wide-eyed Jason as he charged inside with Vern Peterson in tow.

Peterson, however, wasn't nearly as thrilled.

"Yeah," he said suspiciously, looking straight at Farrell. "What's been going on here?"

Kate and Farrell looked at each other. They were both thinking of the threat Peterson had made when Kate had gotten Farrell out of jail. Any more trouble and Farrell had to leave.

CHAPTER FIVE

Farrell straightened and faced the suspicious lawman.

"These fellas were trying to get a little exercise, Sheriff," he said smoothly. "They just seem to have gotten a little carried away," he added, giving a significant glance around the store.

Sheriff Peterson pushed back the brim of his hat and gave the gambler a skeptical look.

"Exercise?" he asked dubiously, looking over the mess.

Just about then the back door opened and Tad and Deke came in with T. J. Walker not too far behind. The boys stopped dead and their mouths fell open, aghast.

"Oh, brother, is Mom ever gonna get us for this!" Tad wailed mournfully as he took in the overturned chairs, cracked table, scattered goods, and general mess.

"What happened?" cried Deke.

The Walker hands had been slowly coming around and staggering to their feet in the meantime. Crowley, still rubbing the back of his head, stepped up and began to speak.

"Exercise, hell!" he exclaimed. "Why, Sheriff, we was just mindin' our own business when Farrell here made a nasty comment about Roebuck's ancestors. Guess he's still sore he couldn't get outa town with them winnings he cheated folks out of a few weeks back," he added, trying for a tone of close friendship with the lawman.

Peterson listened without visible reaction.

"Is that the way it happened?" asked the sheriff, turning his attention to the tall, lanky Roebuck.

Roebuck stuffed his shirt back into his weather-beaten pants.

"Yeah," he muttered, giving Farrell a dark look. "I was just standin' there rollin' my own," he added, nodding toward the remains of his tobacco and cigarette paper on the counter. "He had no cause to say nothin' like that. Why, he was beggin' for a fight!"

Walker watched the tense little scene through narrowed eyes. He decided to stay out of it for the present. Better to let Farrell hang himself . . . just give him enough rope and sooner or later the sheriff would run him out of town if Kate didn't first. To his surprise, Kate came forward in Farrell's defense, instead.

"I wasn't here when all this started, Vern, but I find it hard to believe these five boys all had to jump on Matt in order to defend the honor of Roebuck's forebears, assuming that actually happened!" she said heatedly. "Farrell's been a perfect gentleman the whole time he's been at our place," she added with conviction before casting a hostile glance in Crowley's direction. "That's more than I can say about you in the years that we've been acquainted, Crowley!"

Peterson listened and tried to figure out what was really at the bottom of all this. It didn't make any sense at all to him that a man would goad someone into a fight for no reason . . . and in the presence of four of the man's sidekicks at that! He somehow didn't figure the gambler to be that stupid. Stubborn maybe . . . stupid no.

"You boys have any idea what happened here?" he asked, directing his inquiry to the Johnson kids.

They both shook their heads and simultaneously replied, "No, sir."

"You want to press charges?" he asked.

Tad and Deke looked at each other uncomfortably. Press charges against Walker ranch hands while T.J. was standing by clearly not upset by their having been in a fight? Tad and Deke weren't about to do that! On the other hand, they didn't want to press charges against the gambler, either. They liked Farrell and they knew their mother did too. And it was quite obvious that Kate was going to stand by the gambler. But the store looked like a cyclone had hit one end of it . . . and the Johnsons didn't have enough money to ignore the cost of repairing and replacing damaged goods.

"Gosh, Sheriff," Tad replied awkwardly, "I don't know what to do. . . . Maybe we better go get Mom. . . ." The way his voice trailed off it was obvious that he'd rather go looking for a wounded mountain lion.

Kate marched over to T.J. Hands on hips defiantly, she looked daggers at him and then breathed fire.

"These are your men, T.J. And it was one heck of a coincidence that you and I and Tad and Deke *all* were out of the store when this fracas started. If you ask me, that's just too coincidental to be believed!"

T.J. put up his hands in defense.

"Easy there, Katie girl!" he protested in open-eyed surprise. "You're leapin' to conclusions, honey! I don't know anything about this."

Kate glared at him.

"In a pig's eye!" she exclaimed. "Why there's not a thing your boys do when they're working for you that you don't know about . . . inside and out!"

The sheriff, who had been listening with interest, had to agree with Kate on that. However, agreeing and having evidence were two different things.

"You want to press charges?" he asked bluntly, looking at Farrell first.

That's all I need, Farrell thought. That would tie me up in court . . . assuming Still Waters even had a court, he added cynically. No. He preferred to mete out his own justice.

"No, Sheriff. I figure I made my point." He gave an appreciative smile to Kate and her father. "With a little help from my friends."

The sheriff nodded. He hadn't met many gamblers who liked to get involved with the law. They seemed to prefer their own ways of getting even.

"How 'bout you boys?" Peterson inquired, looking at each of the Walker ranch hands.

They shuffled awkwardly. All of them looked at Crowley. Crowley looked at Walker.

"What do you think, Mr. Walker?" he asked.

T.J. stepped forward and clapped an arm around Crowley's shoulder.

"Well . . . some things are better just forgotten, I reckon," he said in an expansive voice. "Why don't we all just try to forgive and forget?"

He smiled at Kate, who was gaping at him in surprise. If there was one thing she never associated with T.J. it was generosity. He was more selfish and self-centered than anyone she'd ever met. He was up to something!

"Don't you agree, Katie?" he asked, giving her a very warm, very intimate grin.

Kate whirled on her heel and marched stiffly toward the door.

"I couldn't agree with you more, T.J."

"But someone should help pay for the damages," Peterson reminded them, ignoring the fact that no one from the store was pressing for that yet. Peterson liked the Johnsons. He didn't want them to get the short end of the stick merely because they were caught in someone else's feud.

Tad and Deke looked anxiously at their customers. They'd take any help they could get. Anything to soothe their sure-to-be-angry mother!

And with that T.J. saw his opening.

"Yeah, Sheriff. You sure do have a point there. Someone ought to pay up. These folks have had the General Store runnin' without a hitch for quite a long while. They sure shouldn't have to suffer every time some outsider stirs up trouble," he said blandly. "Yep. Someone sure ought to pay."

The sheriff got Walker's message loud and clear, and so did everyone else in the room. All eyes were suddenly on Farrell, who lounged against the front counter flipping a nickel with one hand. Peterson shifted uncomfortably from one foot to the other. He had no interest in railroading Farrell. On the other hand, he had no interest in running up against T.J. on the drifter's account. Especially when he'd warned Farrell that he'd have to face the music if there were any more problems in Still Waters while Farrell was around.

Kate watched Vern's jaw begin to push forward and his fingers begin nervously to snap the loose end of his belt. Ever since he was big enough to wear a belt he'd done the same thing whenever he was trying to find the nerve to take on something he didn't really want to do. Before he could say or do something that would make Farrell's position even more difficult, she had to act.

Kate stepped up to the counter and reached for a pen.

"I'll sign for the damages, Tad," she announced briskly.

T.J.'s mouth fell open in astonishment. He certainly hadn't

expected this. Where in the devil could Kate scrape up the money now, anyhow? He and his father had squeezed her hard for over a year.

Tad, red-faced with embarrassment but too scared to refuse her offer, tore a sheet of paper off a pad and handed it to Kate.

"I owe you," she said aloud as she wrote. Kate looked up calmly and asked, "How much would you say, Tad?"

Tad looked around and did some quick calculations. He'd been helping run the store practically since he was big enough to walk, so he had a fair idea how much things cost.

"I'd say about a hundred and fifty dollars, Miz McKendrick," he said apologetically.

Kate was beginning to write in the amount when Farrell's hand clamped over her wrist, immobilizing it. She looked up at him in surprise. He held her gently, but there was an unbending determination that was transmitted to her all the same.

She looked from his hand to his face in genuine surprise. She *had* to pay! There was no other way out of this for them, as far as she could see. Kate wasn't about to have him suffer more for this. And if he was entertaining some ridiculous masculine notion about not letting a woman pay . . . !

Even as her ire began to rise defensively, another feeling pressed against it. He was staring down at her enigmatically, but there was a warmth in his face . . . in his eyes . . . that made her feel a little weak in the knees for some reason.

"I won't let them do this," she said intensely, her voice low so that only he could hear.

He just kept looking at her as he pulled his wallet out of his hip pocket and removed two bills. He slapped them down on top of the I.O.U.

Kate watched blankly. When her eyes looked into his again, he was still gazing at her in that hooded, hard-to-read way. His hand was like a lover's she thought vaguely. It was tender and protective at the same time. The unbidden image brought a blush to her cheeks, and she shook her head as if to chase it away.

"That won't be necessary," Farrell said. "I'll take care of it." He picked up the note she'd been about to sign and tore it into small pieces. "Thanks for being willing to do it, though," he added, so quietly that only Kate heard him. Only Kate had been meant to hear.

T.J., looking mightily disgruntled, strode toward the door, his hired help falling in behind. He had no idea where Farrell could have come up with two one-hundred-dollar bills, but the way things were going today, he figured he'd be better off not asking. So far every play of the hand had gone Farrell's way. T.J. was a strong believer in the old saying that when the cards were going against you, you might just as well fold 'em and go on home. He gave Kate a cool nod and Farrell a cold stare on his way out.

Of course he had every intention of coming back to play another day. Then maybe the cards would be going *his* way. . . .

"Come on, boys . . . it's time we were gettin' back to the ranch," he drawled. "See you folks later."

Farrell hoisted the sack of feed up onto his shoulder and headed for the door.

"Just a minute, Farrell," the sheriff said, stepping in front of the gambler before he could leave. "Just where did you come by two hundred-dollar bills?"

Farrell shrugged.

"Same way as everybody else, Sheriff," he replied evenly. "I worked for it."

Farrell stared levelly back at the uncertain lawman. Peterson stepped reluctantly aside. He couldn't think of any grounds to pick Farrell up, but he didn't quite trust the gambler. He resented a man who could walk into a town and do as he pleased, not having to bow down to anyone.

But he admired it, too, he had to admit as he watched Farrell carry the grain out to the buckboard and heave it into the back.

"I wish I knew more about him," he said quietly.

Kate, who'd been helping the Johnson boys pick up the mess, heard Peterson's comment.

"Me too," she murmured as she watched Farrell return and begin picking up overturned chairs. "Me too."

"Come help me wash the dishes, Jason," Kate said later that evening as she cleared away the last cups and saucers from the dining-room table.

Jason scampered down from his chair and ran into the kitchen.

"Can I make the soap suds?" he hollered in excitement.

Kate laughed and got out the detergent.

"Sure, sweetie."

The men went into the parlor and stretched out their legs in front of the fireplace.

"Kate sure is a good cook," Loren observed as he lit his pipe. Farrell nodded his head in agreement.

"Don't know how she does as much around here as she does," her father-in-law went on thoughtfully. "She's up at sunup and works till everyone's asleep." He dropped one hand down next to the side of his easy chair and scratched Doc's waiting head. "Guess it's that fierce love of hers."

"People can do more than you think they can when they want to badly enough," Farrell replied enigmatically.

Loren looked at Farrell speculatively.

"That's true. Tell me, you ever want somethin' so bad you'd do anything for it?"

Farrell stared sightlessly into the fire. He felt comfortable talking to McKendrick. They'd developed an unspoken trust over the past few weeks. So Farrell gave McKendrick a real answer instead of the brush-off that was his usual response to personal questions.

"Oh . . . once or twice, I guess."

McKendrick puffed on his pipe, letting the silence work on Farrell a little.

"My mother wanted a new pair of shoes one winter," the gambler recalled. "I was thirteen. For once I saw how she was suffering . . . how much she'd been sacrificing for me. . . . Her shoes had holes in the bottoms and were held together with tape and rubber bands!" He snorted in embarrassment and well-remembered sadness. "So I worked cutting extra firewood for the school in the little town where we were living. I was so tired, I couldn't study. Nearly flunked half my subjects one grading period, but I scraped together enough money to buy her some new shoes."

McKendrick nodded impassively. After all, men weren't supposed to get too emotional about things like that, but Farrell saw the strong sympathy in those old eyes.

And then there was the time he'd spent tracking down his natural father. . . . It had taken him five years, but it had been worth it. At last he'd found the man who'd let his mother struggle all those years alone . . . and soon he was going to have his revenge. He wasn't going to tell McKendrick about that, though . . . that was a little too personal . . . and too close.

McKendrick sensed that Farrell wasn't going to say any more on that topic, even though there was an air about the man that hinted there was a lot more to say. McKendrick let it be. He would respect Farrell's privacy. He scratched Doc's ears and the dog twisted his head and closed his eyes in pleasure.

"Did Jason tell you how we got Doc here?" McKendrick asked.

"No."

"Some rancher had more pups than he wanted to raise, so he dropped Doc here in a river with a rock tied to his neck. Kate saw him when she was out tendin' cattle. That cussed puppy'd struggled to the edge of the bank. How he managed to fight the current and avoid drowning, we've never been able to figure! But he did. When she picked him up he was half drowned and hated every person who tried to touch him. Took Kate over a month to win his trust enough to start trainin' him."

Farrell smiled faintly.

"I can see why he's slow to make friends."

McKendrick grunted agreement.

"Why'd you call him Doc?" Farrell asked curiously.

McKendrick eyed the gambler in amusement.

"After my favorite card game . . . Dr. Pepper."

Farrell looked at the older man in surprise. Then a slow grin spread across his features.

"That's a poker game," he pointed out.

"Yep."

"Like to play a hand?"

McKendrick grinned.

"I thought you'd never get around to askin'!"

Kate walked into the room, drying her hands on a dish towel just as Loren broke out the playing cards.

"Mind if I join you guys?" she asked.

The men answered by drawing up a chair between them at the small card table.

"What are the stakes?" she asked innocently as Farrell shuffled.

"How about penny ante . . . a penny to raise . . . two cents to call?" Loren suggested.

"Sounds fine to me," Farrell said agreeably as he began dealing cards. He watched in fascination as Kate's slender fingers lifted the cards in front of her. "Just fine."

"Well, that about cleans me out," Loren observed a couple of hours later. "I think I'll call it a night."

Farrell gathered the cards and placed the neatly stacked pile in front of him.

"Looks like you're the big winner, boss," he noted in amusement as Kate raked in the huge piles of pennies and began counting them.

"Looks like," she agreed smugly. A teasing glint shone in her eyes. "I had no idea I had such a talent for poker."

Farrell laughed and pushed back his chair.

"Yeah . . . and I was born yesterday," he retorted with a friendly grin.

The sound of Loren's footsteps faded down the hall just before his door closed tight. Farrell and Kate were alone. Only the crackle and snap of the fire broke the silence.

Farrell knew it was late, but he didn't want to leave yet. He lingered, resting a booted foot on the fireplace bricks, pushing a log with an old iron fire poker.

"Has it started to snow yet?" he asked, glancing over his shoulder to see Kate staring out the window overlooking the porch.

She shook her head.

"No. Maybe later tonight. By tomorrow morning for certain."

The silence enfolded them again. Kate joined Farrell near the fireplace.

"Would you mind if I asked you a question?" Farrell asked soberly.

"Of course not," Kate replied.

"How were you planning on coming up with that hundred and fifty dollars when you signed that IOU this morning?"

He wasn't looking at her, but she felt the seriousness behind the question. Kate took a deep breath.

"I don't know."

He poked a burning coal. A shower of red embers rose up into the chimney along with the hot air and smoke.

"That's what I thought," he murmured.

Farrell hung the poker on a hook next to the fireplace and covered the opening with the screen. Then he turned to look at Kate.

"You know . . . you're the only stranger who ever made an effort to go to bat for me, Kate McKendrick."

Kate gazed at him, mesmerized by the play of gold and red light over his face. The firelight cast shadows over his features, accentuating the angular planes and strong lines . . . adding warmth and intimacy.

"I wouldn't say you're a stranger anymore," she argued, a little faintly. Why did she feel that peculiar weakness overtaking her again?

He studied her, trying to hold back his thoughts. Something about her pulled them out of him, though. He couldn't seem to stop himself.

"No . . . I guess we aren't exactly strangers anymore," he agreed softly. "But you don't know much about me, Kate. Certainly not as much as most people want to know before they plunk down that much hard cash . . . especially when it's as hard for them to scrape together as it is for you right now."

"I know you well enough," she argued. "I trust my own judgment of people, remember? And in the time you've been here you've been hardworking, loyal, patient, and a very good person, Matt Farrell!" Her voice grew fiercer and more emphatic with every word.

Farrell gazed at her, lingering over her glowing features with a longing that had been growing stronger every day. He wanted to reach out and touch her . . . to trace the silky curve of her cheek . . . the soft skin of her throat . . . the graceful shape of her back and hips. . . .

He shook his head slightly.

Forget it, Farrell. She's too good for you. . . . She'd cringe if you even made a move toward her. Who are you, anyway? A man who lays his entire bankroll on the line in a game of

90

chance? A man who isn't considered decent for polite society or hardworking folk to socialize with? A bastard . . . in the literal sense of the word?

But he couldn't rid himself of the longing for her . . . to touch her . . . just once . . . would be so sweet . . . so sweet. . . .

He started to walk toward the door. Kate was engulfed in a wave of disappointment. She thought quickly. How could she keep him here a little while longer?

"I want to thank you, Matt," she said in a rush.

He stopped and turned to look at her in puzzlement.

"Thank me? For what?"

"You've worked so hard for us. Much harder than room and board are worth around here. And I'm sure there are other things you could have done that would have paid good money. . . ." Her voice trailed off. She was suddenly afraid that by mentioning those unknown "other things" he might decide to take off and pursue them.

Kate, she castigated herself, think before you talk!

He was looking at her in a strange way. That poker face had slipped over his handsome features again, she noted. But there was a light in his eyes she hadn't noticed before . . . like a hunger or a yearning for something. . . . Her heart melted a little more. She wanted to ease the yearning, but she couldn't quite bring herself to find out what it was. There was an air about him that frightened her a little. Instinctively she felt the masculine aura. The female in her made her wary of him. And yet . . . she didn't want him to go.

"If I worked hard, it was because I wanted to, Kate. And as far as I'm concerned, living with you and your family has been the best pay I ever got."

She looked at him in disbelief.

"It's true," he insisted with a shrug. "You wouldn't know. You've always had a home, roots, a family. For someone like me, sleeping in a homestead that's been a haven for several generations . . . eating home-cooked meals . . . playing with a little boy . . . swapping stories with a grandfather . . . how can you put a price tag on things like that?"

Kate's tender heart ached for him and for all the unhappiness

91

of his childhood and youth. She reached out and touched his shoulder, as if trying to ease the hurt somehow.

"I'm glad we could give you that at least, Matt," she said softly. "And I hope you'll stay and enjoy it for as long as you like."

"That's a rash offer, lady," he said huskily.

He couldn't tear his eyes away from her. He was lost in their hidden emerald depths. Drowning in them. The soft touch of her hand on his arm was increasing his heart rate unbelievably. All he could think of was how he wished that soft hand would wind around his neck. . . . How he was tempted to pull her close . . . just once.

He stepped back and her arm fell down to her side. When he saw the wounded look in her eyes, fleeting as it was, he could have kicked himself. He hadn't meant her to feel rejected. It was just that he wasn't sure how much of her closeness he could take anymore without acting on his impulses.

"Are you going to be able to make it through the winter here without hired help of some sort?" he asked neutrally, trying to redirect their conversation to a less personal level.

Kate lifted her chin.

"We'll make it," she vowed.

"And if the Walkers manage to prevent you from selling or shipping your beef in the next twelve months?" he asked.

"It'll be very tough," she conceded. "But don't forget . . . I have more than cattle ranching in mind as a livelihood. . . . I don't want all my eggs in one basket if I can help it!"

"Ah, yes," he acknowledged, smiling faintly. "Your ace in the hole."

Kate didn't want to think how they'd manage if that didn't work. She knew that Farrell wouldn't drop it at that. So she was ready for his next question when it came.

"And if that fails?" he inquired gently.

Kate paced around the furniture and looked out the window again.

"Well . . . I used to guide hunters through the mountains around here when I was a teenager. I could do it again."

He frowned and stared at the floor.

"Just why are the Walkers so determined to squeeze you out, Kate?"

"I wish I knew," she sighed. "Ever since I was a kid T.J.'s wanted to be the big man about town. His father never misses a chance to turn a profit or acquire landholdings around here." She lifted her shoulders and shook her head in a gesture of exasperation. "Maybe we're just an obstacle to those ambitions."

Farrell listened thoughtfully.

"But it must be costing them . . . if only in terms of favors owed at a later date," he mused. "Have they bought out all the surrounding ranches? Are you a holdout? The only missing piece of a puzzle for some big land development scheme?" he asked.

Kate shook her head.

"No. There's the Peterson ranch and the church holdings along the north end of town . . . the Johnson ranch abuts the south side of town . . . a big spread owned by some Los Angeles corporation cuts off one corner of the Walker ranch from another property that the Major holds the mortgage on. . . . No. If I wanted just to expand the town limits, or extend the Walker ranch boundaries, or build a solid empire of land holdings, there are several other sections I'd be trying hard to get my hands on," she replied.

"Then why else could they be doing it?" he asked. Perhaps he'd feel better about leaving her here if he knew just what she was up against. Maybe he could even find some way to help her out. The picture of Kate having to stand up to the Walkers alone had become less and less tolerable to him with every passing day.

Kate sighed and grimaced. A slight blush crept into her cheeks.

"Well, if you want to believe T.J.'s explanation . . . the one he's managed to convince Vern Peterson and a few other people to believe . . . it's because he's madly in love with me and his father wants to help him court me by taking the roof from over my head!" she said with a laugh. "I don't know why anyone would take that feeble argument seriously. I can hardly keep a straight face when I hear it! Besides, it's common knowledge that Sissy Wells would scratch the eyes out of any woman who got in her way with T.J."

Farrell grinned faintly.

"That's going to great lengths, all right," he said, although he wasn't laughing at it. It wasn't all *that* incredible to him, actually. "Some men have been known to go to great lengths, however," he added.

Kate gave him a measuring look.

"Is that so? Would you do something like that, Farrell?" she asked. She faced him, interested in his reply.

Farrell walked over to the fireplace and poked at the embers again.

"Nope," he said. "But I'm a gambler," he reminded her coolly. "Gamblers lose their edge when they get too attached to their possessions . . . or when they have a family depending on them to keep food on the table"—he gave her a sidewise glance—"or a roof over their heads."

Kate was dismayed to feel the disappointment his words brought to her. Why should it bother her? she asked herself. What difference did it make? She knew he wasn't going to stay here forever. After all, a professional gambler could hardly make a living in Still Waters. You needed to travel for that . . . to Reno and Las Vegas and lots of other places.

She stiffened her resolve and forced herself to carry on the conversation as if his remark hadn't hurt a little.

"Okay. You're not the kind of man to do something like that. But it doesn't make sense to me that T.J. or his father are so wildly eager to have me in the family that they'd go to these lengths to do it!"

Farrell leaned his shoulder against the wall next to the fireplace and rested the tip of the poker against the bricks.

"Oh, I don't know, Kate. Men have been known to come up with some pretty wild schemes when they're trying to capture the affection of a woman." He grinned. "Take the case of Helen of Troy, for example."

Kate laughed and put her hands on her hips.

"Come on, Farrell! I'm no Helen and this is most definitely not Troy!"

Farrell dipped his head in acknowledgment of her retort, but the peculiar gleam in his dark eyes made her wonder what he was really thinking. And why he wasn't saying it out loud.

"Maybe not," he agreed. "So . . . why else could they be

going to these lengths? Is your land worth more than everyone else's?"

"Not especially." Kate grew serious. "I've looked at it from every angle, Farrell, and for the life of me I can't figure it out. We have a lot of land. True. When my sister and her husband got a good start in San Francisco, my folks had trouble keeping up their ranch. My dad was getting too old to run it alone. So they moved to San Francisco and Seth and I agreed to keep the place up."

Seth. It was the first time Farrell had ever heard her speak her husband's name. He heard it with mixed feelings. He didn't really want to get to know much about her husband, he realized in surprise. It was easier not to think of her with another man. Even in the past.

"Now my sister really has her hands full," Kate went on. "My father had a stroke two years ago. He's partially paralyzed. My mother takes care of him, but they're living in my sister's home. They've had their hands full out there."

She realized how much she was drifting into her family's life story and waved a hand as if to dismiss it.

"Sorry. That's not exactly the point," she said, embarrassed. "Anyway . . . we have a lot of good grazing land, some excellent stands of timber in the foothills, and good water from a couple of creeks that cut through our property. But we're not unique. Lots of people have ranches that could be described like that."

"Hm." Farrell shook his head. "There must be something—"

"Oh, look!" Kate cried softly, hurrying over to draw back the lace curtain and pointing outside. "The first snow!"

Farrell joined her. A light dusting of flakes was falling gently across the darkened land as far as the eye could see.

"When I was little I would pretend it was fairy dust, spreading magic wherever it fell," she reminisced.

Farrell, staring out the window from just behind her, saw the dreamy, faraway look reflected in her eyes. He envied the memories she had.

"For your sake, I hope it is fairy dust. I have the feeling you're going to need all the luck you can get this winter." He shoved a hand in his back pocket, searching for the key to the old homestead. "I guess I'd better be going."

"Yes, of course." Kate tried to pull herself back into the role of boss and owner of the ranch, but their relationship had changed. She helped him on with his coat. They stood in the parlor, each trying to find the will to say good-bye.

Farrell wondered what in the world had happened to him. He could feel her hands through the heavy material almost as if it were as thin as lace. He tried to think about something else, but his mind would not cooperate. She was standing so close to him, he could catch the scent of her and it sent a flash of desire through him before he could do anything about it.

"Well, thanks again," he said awkwardly, turning grimly toward the door and ordering his feet to march toward it.

Kate bit her lip. She didn't want him to leave. Oh, how she didn't want him to! But for the life of her, she couldn't think of a reason for him to stay! The coy things women say to men just couldn't come out of her mouth. It brought a tinge of color to her cheeks to think that he might actually guess her inner turmoil! That wouldn't do. She racked her brain for a subject. Anything to keep his solid, welcome presence near her just a little longer . . .

"Oh, by the way," she blurted out in relief, hurrying after him and praying that something would come to her.

Farrell stopped instantly.

"Yes?" he prompted her, fastening his eyes on her in an agony of conflicting feelings.

He kept telling himself to go, but he was dying to stay. He felt like a marionette, reluctantly willing to let her pull his strings, even though he steadfastly refused to impose himself on her. He told himself he must be nuts to subject himself to this exquisitely painful pleasure. He took a deep breath and waited grimly for Kate to continue.

"I, uh . . ." She stumbled over the words as she tried desperately to think of something else to say. Farrell was staring at her intently. "I've been meaning to ask. Why *did* those Walker ranch hands pick a fight with you this morning?"

She would have applauded her own ingenuity if it hadn't been a dead giveaway of how hard it was for her to call an end to the evening. Instead, she managed a casual air of curiosity.

"They were trying to convince me to seek employment in another town," Farrell replied dryly.

"That makes twice, doesn't it?"

Farrell nodded. She believed him, he thought. It was good to know.

"Yes," he said. "I'm pretty sure they were the ones that beat me up the first time too. Of course I doubt I could ever prove it."

Kate frowned and bit her lower lip thoughtfully.

"Maybe this time they tried to chase you off because you were helping me, Farrell," she suggested unhappily.

He touched her chin lightly with the fingertips of one hand.

"Hey," he said softly, "maybe they're just sore losers."

She looked into his eyes. They were the warmest, richest shade of hazel, she thought. And very distracting to look at.

"You don't believe that any more than I do," she murmured.

He shrugged and pulled away from her.

"Don't worry about it, boss." He gave her a crooked grin. "The troops arrived in the nick of time."

This time he forced himself to open the door.

"See you tomorrow."

"Good night, Farrell."

Samuel Walker poured a brandy from the crystal decanter before replacing it in the antique cabinet behind him. He swirled the rich amber liquid slowly in the snifter.

"I hear Farrell is still at the McKendrick ranch," he said.

T.J. walked angrily across the room and poured himself the same.

"Don't worry about Farrell," the younger Walker growled. "One way or the other, I'll take care of him."

Samuel inhaled the fragrant bouquet of the drink in his hand.

"I don't want anything to spoil my plans, T.J.," he said in the tough iron-willed voice that had been the death knell for many a business adversary over the years.

"I said don't worry about him!" T.J. exclaimed angrily.

"The same goes for Kate." Samuel sighed regretfully. "But try to make sure she isn't hurt in the process. I've always admired that girl."

T.J. drained his brandy in one gulp.

"I'll take care of Kate," he said as anger darkened his face. "Personally."

Samuel watched his son's face harden into a cruel expression. "Just see to it she isn't hurt," Samuel ordered.

CHAPTER SIX

Farrell knew he had to leave.

The game waiting for him in Reno next week represented a once-in-a-lifetime chance. He'd planned for too long to drop it now.

Grim-faced, he finished pounding the fence into shape. After he repaired the fence behind the corral he was going to tell Kate it was time for him to leave.

"Matt! Matt!" cried a high little voice. Jason ran toward him at full tilt. "There's a phone call for you!" He climbed onto the bottom slat. "Can I help?" he asked hopefully.

Farrell shoved the piece of wood into place and looked down at the eager little boy.

"Sure, kid," he said with a grin. He patted Jason's head affectionately. "After I answer the phone." They walked back to the house together. "Do you know who it is?" he asked.

Jason frowned, trying hard to remember.

"Mr. Maybury?" he mumbled hesitantly. He gave Farrell a doubtful look.

Farrell didn't know any Mayburys. Then a possibility occured to him.

"Mr. Mallory?"

Jason's face lit up with relief.

"That's it!" he crowed cheerily. Then he began running as fast as his little legs would carry him up the hill toward the main house. "I'm gonna beat ya!" he shouted gaily.

"That's no fair! You gave yourself a head start, short-stuff!" Farrell shouted with mock outrage. He counted to five, then loped up the hillside after the miniature tornado in winter gear.

Kate had ridden out early to check the fence along the western ridge. The snowfall had been light. Calamity loped easily through the small accumulation while Kate enjoyed the beautiful view.

The view of the fence wasn't as enchanting, unfortunately.

"That looks like an elephant ran through it!" she exclaimed. She patted the mare on the neck and surveyed the damage from the saddle. "Looks like I'll be mending fence this week, Calamity."

There were no tracks in the snow. Whatever had happened had occurred before it fell. Whatever clues there might have been were buried under a white blanket.

Kate clucked softly and gave the reins a gentle pull.

"Let's go down and see if the cattle are where we left 'em!"

And then go home and see if Farrell is still there.

"Mom! Mom!"

Jason ran out to greet Kate. She reached down and swung him up into the saddle in front of her. Calamity lowered her head and snorted in long-suffering forbearance.

"I helped Matt fix the fence," he said excitedly. "He said I did real good!"

Kate gave her little bundle of energy a hug and kissed his cheek.

"You're getting to be quite a helper, Jason!" she laughed.

"Can I go out and help you with the cattle tomorrow, Mom? Please?"

Kate let the mare walk into the barn. She dismounted inside and Jason quickly jumped down after her.

"Sure, honey," she said. "How about loosening Calamity's cinch? She's already pretty cooled down."

"Okay. Oh. And guess what? A man called Matt and told him he'd give him a ride to Reno!"

Kate's head snapped up.

"Is that so?"

She lifted off the saddle and unfastened the bridle.

"I wish he wouldn't go," Jason said wistfully. "I liked him bein' here."

Kate slipped the halter over the mare's head and began currying her.

"Did he say when he was going, Jason?" she asked.

"Tomorrow."

Kate's hand stopped in mid-stroke.

"Tomorrow?" she repeated.

Even though she'd known he'd eventually go, the news stunned her. Now it was real.

"Jason says you're planning on leaving tomorrow," she said.

Farrell hadn't heard her approach. He turned, startled.

"Yes."

They were standing by the fence he'd been working on. He motioned awkwardly toward it.

"This'll be finished. And the work inside the barn."

She thought it sounded like an apology. Funny. She didn't think of Farrell as the type of man to offer a justification for what he did or apologize for not doing more.

"You've done more than I ever dreamed you would," she said. Why did she feel so awful, she wondered unhappily. She looked over the work he'd done. "Maybe you should consider being a carpenter if you ever get tired of gambling," she joked. "This is good work."

"I learned it on the job as a kid," he said vaguely.

Kate tilted her head and smiled at him.

"You sure are a jack-of-all-trades, Matt Farrell. And on behalf of all the McKendricks, I'd like to thank you." She held out her hand. "You've done more for us than a lot of people I've known all my life. I thank you."

Reluctantly he shook hands with her. He didn't want to do it. As soon as his fingers closed over hers he knew he'd been right to want to avoid it. A sizzling current of awareness shot across his palm and lightninged through his body.

Kate felt a rush of pleasure as his hazel eyes gazed enigmatically into hers. Heat seared her palm where it touched his. Her chest tightened painfully; she was holding her breath.

Breathe, darn it! she ordered herself. You're not a schoolgirl! You aren't the type to swoon at a man's feet, either!

She swallowed and pulled her hand away.

"Well . . . you're always welcome to stop by when you're traveling through, Farrell," she said, forcing every word out of her mouth and doing her darnedest to make it sound natural.

"Thanks." He gripped the fence post with one hand. "And if you ever come to Reno, look me up. Maybe I can keep you from getting fleeced," he added with a grin.

She smiled awkwardly. Damn! Why did they have to be standing here like this? Not knowing what to say to each other? Like two strangers. It was as if there were an unseen barrier between them, holding them apart. Kate lifted her chin and smiled her best and brightest smile.

"See you at dinner, then," she said.

Farrell watched her straight back disappear around the barn as she marched up to the house with firm, rapid steps. She had a kindness in her that made him hunger for more. But it was obvious to him that she wasn't going to miss him when he was gone. She might miss the help, he conceded. But she wasn't going to ache for him.

Farrell had the sinking feeling that he couldn't say the same for himself. He slapped the rough wood of the fence post with his open hand. Damn! Why did he have to run into her? His life had been so much clearer before. He'd known exactly what he wanted and how he was going to get it. And he'd been willing to pay the price to reach his goal.

He looked up at the foothills that rose up along the back of the ranch. Every time he saw a mountain or a pine or a ranch, he knew he was going to think of her.

Angrily he hit the post with his fist.

"I'm my own man!" he muttered. "She's just a woman, damn it. You see them all the time. All over the place. The world's thick with them, for crying out loud!"

He kept telling himself that. Over and over.

Mallory pulled up in front of the McKendricks' house late Friday afternoon. Jason, as usual, was excited that company had come to call. He was oblivious of the strain between his mother and Matt. They'd barely spoken to each other since Farrell had announced he was leaving. Kate had hitched up the buckboard at dawn and had spent hours repairing the fence she'd discovered broken down the previous morning. She'd returned close to dark, dead tired, falling into bed immediately after dinner.

Farrell had made himself equally scarce, avoiding the house as if afraid Kate might suddenly return. He'd repaired a small section of roof on the old homestead that had begun to leak; then he'd chopped enough wood to last them a month. Jason, busy with his own chores, had noticed nothing odd.

But Loren had noticed.

"I'd like to thank you for all the hard work you put in here, Matt," he said as Farrell came to say good-bye.

The two men shook hands.

McKendrick leaned on his cane.

"If you find things don't look the way you remember them when you get to Reno, you're welcome to come for a visit," he said solemnly.

Farrell was taken by surprise. He hadn't expected a personal invitation from the McKendricks. Especially from Loren.

"It's all a matter of what you want out of life," the older man explained with a philosophical shrug. "Sometimes it takes a while to find out what that is," he added.

Matt nodded, although he couldn't figure out why McKendrick was philosophizing or exactly what was meant by the comment.

"Matt!" Jason shrieked as he hurled himself into the gambler's arms. Fortunately for Jason, Matt had quick reflexes and caught the little boy. "It's almost Thanksgiving! Please come to our house for Thanksgiving! Please!" he pleaded.

Farrell glanced sharply at Kate, who was standing on the porch steps nearby. She looked as surprised as he by the sudden invitation.

"I don't think—" he began.

"It's all right," Jason interrupted, desperately searching for a powerful ally. "Mom doesn't mind, do you, Mom?"

Kate looked at his anxious little face. Her heart twisted. She wanted Farrell to come and yet she was afraid to have him around. It was the tension . . . the invisible barrier. . . . She looked at Farrell. Damn the barbed-wire wall that had mysteriously appeared between them! She'd just have to deal with that.

"I'd be happy to have him," she said simply.

Farrell's eyes locked with hers.

"Will you, Matt? Will you?"

He had to return to win his money back from Walker, he

reminded himself. Why not stay with the McKendricks? Probably no one else around here would rent him a room for the night, anyway, he argued. And he'd get to see her, one last time. . . . It was too tempting to pass up.

"All right," he agreed. "Thank you."

Jason bounced up and down and whooped and hollered. His noise and antics covered the deafening silence between Kate and Matt.

"I hate to put an end to this," Amos said, "but we'd better get started. I've got to be in Reno tonight. It was nice meeting you folks again," he added sincerely.

As the two men got into the car Kate was again struck by Amos Mallory's appearance. There was something so familiar about him. What could it be? she wondered. Mallory and Farrell waved and suddenly she knew what it was.

"Why, they look enough alike to be father and son," she murmured to herself. It was in the strong cheekbones . . . and the crinkles at the corners of their eyes . . . the determined set of the jaw. . . .

"Good-bye, Matt Farrell," she whispered. "See you at Thanksgiving."

"You've been pretty quiet. Even for you," Amos commented after they were well away from Still Waters.

Farrell, lying back against the front seat with his eyes shut, did not reply.

"The McKendricks seem like real nice people," Amos tried again.

"Yeah," came the muttered response.

"Mrs. McKendrick sure is a pretty thing." Amos glanced at his reluctant partner in conversation.

There was a moment of silence. Farrell twisted around a little, trying to find a more comfortable position.

"I didn't notice," he finally mumbled.

Amos raised both eyebrows in amazement. Then he started to chuckle.

"What's so funny?" Matt asked with a trace of irritation.

Amos laughed harder.

"Yeah. I can see you didn't!" he finally managed to say.

Farrell grumbled something about being worn out and wanting to get some shut-eye. Amos wore a grin as wide as the Sierra Nevada all the way back to Reno.

"Hit me."

Another card slithered across the green-felt tabletop. Farrell lifted a corner and slowly added it to his hand.

Amos watched thoughtfully as Farrell picked up a stack of chips and dropped them into the center of the table.

"I'll see that and raise you $10,000."

Mallory pulled out a cheroot and struck a match against the bottom of his shoe. He inhaled slowly, his eyes never leaving the man across the small table from him.

"I'll see your raise with another ten percent share of the casino," he said, pushing forward a small piece of paper. It joined eight other pieces already on the pile. Each was an IOU for ten percent of Mallory's casino, signed in his own hand.

Farrell folded his cards. Beneath the carefully unrevealing face he automatically wore at the poker table, he struggled with the doubts that had been assailing him ever since they'd returned to Reno.

Across the table from him was Amos Mallory, a man who had been a good friend and mentor to him for close to seven years. He'd been like a father to him in many ways, Farrell reluctantly had to admit. Each year Farrell had jokingly challenged Mallory to play for the ultimate high-stakes poker game. The one where you lay everything you have on the line.

For some reason, this year Mallory had agreed.

At first Farrell couldn't believe it. Then he'd tasted triumph. After all these years he was going to destroy the man who'd destroyed his mother's life . . . the man who'd made Farrell's growing up a living hell.

Now it was all within his grasp. Farrell knew he had Mallory. And yet for the past few days there had been no rush of gratification . . . no righteous sense of justice . . . not even the sweet taste of revenge.

There was just that hollow, empty feeling inside.

Farrell didn't want to go through with it. Mallory the man wasn't like the unseen, unknown father that Farrell had hated bitterly for all those years. Instead, he'd turned out to be one hell of a nice guy. A strong, loyal man. A good man.

"I'll call," Mallory said calmly, shoving the last slip onto the pile.

He inhaled again and then slowly blew out a thin stream of smoke. He watched Farrell with a detached interest. That air of distance wasn't like him. Matt wasn't sure exactly what to make of it.

There was $300,000 of Farrell's money lying in the pot. That represented a lot of winning poker hands. It was the fruit of a couple of years of high stakes winnings, the net earnings of a tough-minded professional in a cutthroat business. It had taken guts to stand down that many bets. And it took a lot of card-playing skill.

It was too late to go back now. Someone had to win. Farrell knew that. But for once, he was sick at heart at the prospect.

He pressed his lips together and shook his head. He couldn't go through with it.

"You win," Farrell said, folding his cards facedown in a neat pile.

Mallory stared at him in astonishment. He sat motionless, as if not quite believing what he'd heard. Ash from the cheroot fell onto the table. He brushed it away and put the cheroot, tip-first, into the stone ashtray next to him.

Farrell began to push his chair back.

"Just a minute," he ordered. "I called. I want to see your cards." Before Matt could stop him Amos turned them over and spread them out on the table with a sweep of his hand.

Amos looked up at Farrell. He spread his own cards next to Farrell's.

"Four of a kind beats a full house," Amos pointed out in a soft, steady voice. "You win."

Farrell pushed back his chair and stood up.

"This game was a mistake, Amos. I don't want your casino. Let's just call it quits," Farrell said irritably.

Mallory leaned back in his chair.

"Tell me, Matt. Why the change of heart?" he asked curiously, that same air of detachment clinging to him.

Farrell rubbed the back of his neck.

"I found it wasn't what I thought it would be," he hedged. "What in the hell do I need a casino for, anyway? I'd have to sit around and manage the damn thing."

Mallory nodded his head.

"I see your point." He decided to approach it from a different angle. "Something like that happened to me recently," he said. "Right about the time you got sidetracked in Still Waters, as a matter of fact."

Farrell's sixth sense perked up.

"That so?" he asked warily.

"Yeah. When you didn't show up that Monday and nobody'd heard from you here at the casino, I went over to your apartment at the Nevadan. I talked Cathy into letting me in so I could get some clues on your whereabouts. I was getting a little worried about you."

Farrell stiffened.

"That so?"

"Yeah. Remember when I drove through and stopped to see you at the McKendricks' the first time? I told you I was on my way to Sacramento on business?" When Farrell nodded Amos continued. "Well, I took a little detour by way of Fresno before I came back."

Farrell's head snapped up and his eyes darkened dangerously.

"I'd like to talk to you about it, if you're willing," Mallory said. For the first time the detachment slipped. Mallory looked unsure of himself. "I'd be obliged if you'd give me the chance."

Kate took out the books and forced herself to start adding the columns. It was late at night. Everyone else was asleep. It was the time she always chose to do the bookkeeping. No one had to see how worried she really was. The figures didn't look any better this month than they had the last. If they couldn't get the cash to pay off the bank loan next spring, she'd have to sell some of her land.

She rested her head on her forearms.

She was too exhausted to cry. Besides, crying never helped anyway, she reminded herself fuzzily. She'd just rest her eyes for a few minutes. Then go to bed.

As she drifted off to sleep, slumped over the books, the enigmatic, handsome face of a hard-bitten gambler swam before her. He bent closer, closer . . . until she could almost feel the brush of his lips against hers . . . almost.

Farrell held the old-fashioned glass between the fingertips of one hand and gently swirled the amber-colored liquid over the ice cubes. He took a swallow and savored the blended whiskeys as they burned a path down his throat.

They'd moved from the private back room into the bar. Since it was long past closing time, they were alone. The place was deserted.

Farrell expelled a long, frustrated breath.

"I don't know what to say," he admitted.

Mallory nodded his head.

"I know exactly what you mean. Maybe I should begin. I had a long talk with your mother when I was in Fresno. She'd known I was married, of course. But she never knew why I hadn't shown up for that last meeting." He shook his head sadly. "I'd just found out that my wife was terminally ill. For over a year I'd thought we just weren't getting along. That's why I told her I wanted a separation. It was just after I moved out of the house that I met your mother."

Mallory lit up another cheroot and leaned one elbow against the bar.

"She was the best thing that ever happened to me," Amos said, his voice softening with affection. "But I was so much older than she was . . . I wasn't sure she was as serious about me as I was about her. Besides, my life was pretty much of a mess then, since I was thinking of filing for divorce. That was when the doctor told me my wife's problem was a disease . . . and that it was going to keep getting worse."

Mallory stabbed the ashtray with the cheroot.

"So I, in an effort to be noble about the damn thing, decided to break off with your mother and go back to my wife. I never knew about you. Your mother assumed I was giving her the brush-off," he went on, his voice husky with regret. "She left town and two months later realized she was pregnant. She spent seventeen years struggling to raise you alone while I watched my wife gradually turn into a complete stranger, a shell of the woman I'd married." There was a moment of complete silence as each man nursed his own thoughts. "She died a couple of years before you finally found me," Amos added.

Farrell drained the whiskey.

"You knew I was your son when you picked me up in Still

Waters," Farrell pointed out. "You must have realized why I've been trying to get you into a poker game with the casino as the stakes. Why did you take the gamble?"

Mallory half smiled, but his eyes were sad.

"I'd give everything I have to undo the past thirty-odd years for you, Matt. Before I found out about our relationship, I considered you a son in every way but the legal one. The son I thought I never had. I wanted you to have the casino, Matt."

"And if I'd lost?" asked Farrell, trying to take it all in.

Mallory grinned.

"Why then you'd be broke and looking for a job, a game, or a stake. I'd have supplied any or all of them." He laughed. "With your own money!"

Farrell grinned faintly.

"Win or lose, I'd be stuck here. Is that it?"

Mallory nodded.

"I'd always intended you to have the casino, Matt. About a year ago I had my lawyer draw up a new will and designated that in writing. Yesterday I had him add your mother as well."

Mallory poured them both another drink and raised his glass in a toast.

"To us. May our futures be happier than our pasts."

Farrell stared at his drink, hesitating. Then, slowly, he raised his glass and touched it to Mallory's.

"To happy futures . . ."

They drank and talked quietly for a while, trying to fill in some of the many gaps in the past. When they'd both relaxed a little Amos recalled something else he'd recently discovered.

"By the way," he said, "while you were in Still Waters I did a little checking around to see what I could find out about the McKendricks and the Walkers. I have to admit I was more worried about the Walkers, since it was their card parlor you'd just left when you got beat up."

Farrell perked up noticeably.

"Oh? Find anything interesting?"

"As a matter of fact, I did," Amos acknowledged. He shrugged as if to qualify his statement. "Of course it may just be coincidence . . . but I was talking to a friend of mine who's an assayer here in Nevada. . . ."

"I'll get it!" Kate shouted. She raced to the ringing phone and yanked it off the receiver. "Hello?"

"Hello, Kate."

Kate sagged against the wall and slowly slid down it to the floor. Farrell. The tormenter of her dreams. The ones at night and the ones during the day.

"I hope I haven't called too late," he was saying.

Kate soaked up the husky, rough sound of his voice with a pleasure so profound, so unexpected, that it took her breath away.

"No," she replied weakly. "You didn't."

She couldn't think of a thing to say and she knew she was hanging on to the phone praying that he could. Just like a lovesick adolescent, she thought in dismay. You never outgrow some things, she realized uncomfortably.

Farrell, who'd been strangely silent himself, finally found his voice.

"I have a proposition for you," he said. Hastily he added, "A business proposition."

Kate heard the flush in the change of tone in his voice. She grinned and leaned her head back against the wall.

"I'm listening," she said softly.

There was a hesitation, like he was taking a deep breath before plunging ahead. Kate thought how uncharacteristic that was of the taciturn, tough man she'd plucked out of the Still Waters jail that morning weeks ago. Her expression softened with tenderness.

"You told me you were considering guiding hunters to earn some cash," he reminded her.

"Yes," she agreed, puzzled.

He hesitated for an instant.

"How would you feel about doing that next week for a paying customer?"

"I could," she mused, still taken by surprise at his suggestion. "Who's the hunter and what's he after?" she asked.

"I'm the hunter. And I'd like to explain after I get there." His voice became suspiciously neutral. "Can you trust me that far?"

Kate's lips curved tenderly.

"Sure, Matt. Explain when you get here."

She thought she heard a sigh of relief, but she couldn't be sure. Maybe it's just wishful thinking, she admonished herself.

"I want it clearly understood that this time I'm a paying guest, Kate."

"You don't have to sound so warning, Farrell!" she laughed. "I'm a businesswoman. I know how to take money in exchange for goods or a service!"

"Just so there's no misunderstanding . . ."

This time she heard the half smile in his voice. If she closed her eyes, she could see it too . . . and the rest of him, as well.

"Oh, by the way, do you mind if I bring a few things with me?"

"Not at all."

Bring everything you own, if you like, she impishly added to herself. For some reason she didn't have the nerve to say it out loud. Maybe it was a little too close to the truth.

"Would next Tuesday be too soon?" he asked.

"Not at all." Too soon? He had to be kidding, she thought, trying to slow down her pounding heart and get a grip on herself. "We'll be looking forward to seeing you again," she said as coolly and as politely as she could. She thought the "we" was a nice touch too. It made it sound like she was just one of a crowd.

"Thanks," he said evenly. "See you sometime in the afternoon, then."

Kate got up to hang up the phone. To her surprise she felt as weak as a kitten when she tried to stand.

"Don't add to your problems, Kate," she told herself severely. "So he's an attractive man. The world is full of them!" she muttered to herself.

But there was only one Matt Farrell, her rebellious spirit argued. And he was coming back . . . he was coming back.

"When you said you were bringing a few things, I thought you meant clothes!" Kate laughed as their horses plodded through the snowy landscape a few days later.

He grinned crookedly, glancing at her sideways.

"Much as I would have enjoyed riding double with you on Calamity, I thought we'd cover more ground if we each had a horse."

"Good point," she agreed, looking back at him from half-lowered eyes. "By the way, where'd you get the horse and trailer, anyway? I hardly think of a gambler needing them for transportation these days!"

The horses picked their way through the snow, lifting their hoofs smartly. Their tracks etched a dotted trail as far as the eye could see down the hilly terrain behind them.

"I won them in a card game," Farrell said with a grin.

"I should have guessed!"

"I've been keeping him at Mallory's ranch outside Reno for almost six months, trying to decide what to do with him." He patted the horse's thick gray coat with a gloved hand. "I guess I waited too long, though."

"Why do you say that?" she asked curiously.

Farrell's eyes scanned the timbered ridges rising in all directions around them.

"I got attached to him."

Kate looked away from him.

"What's wrong with that?" she asked stiffly.

Farrell pulled his Stetson down over his eyes a little more.

"A gambler can't afford to get attached to things," he answered bluntly.

"Oh, yes," she said, nodding her head. Her voice had a sharp edge to it. "I forgot. How stupid of me."

She shortened the reins a little and dug her heels into the mare's sides. Calamity leaped forward and took the side of the rising foothills in great bursts of energy.

Farrell leaned forward and gave his horse his head, following suit. The trees were thicker here. They climbed above the once grassy slopes, rimmed with manzanita and buckbrush and occasional clumps of black oak stretching their barren winter branches over the cold, wild landscape now dusted with snow.

Soon the horses were picking their way through tall stands of ponderosa pines, their dark green needles still showing beneath the snowy frosting.

The horses' breathing became labored, and great plumes of steam billowed out in front of them. Kate reluctantly slowed to a steady walk.

"The stream comes down the mountain here," she said briskly, pointing out the partially frozen ribbon of clear silver spilling over the rocks. "It's almost a river in the spring. Late in the winter it's just a thin trickle. Hardly worth calling a creek, I guess."

They stopped and turned to survey the land below them. Kate pointed out the landmarks as she spoke.

"The ranch house is about five miles over that stand of yellow pine you can just barely make out down there along the horizon. The other creek comes down the mountainside about three miles over there, then runs along the other edge of the ranch."

Farrell pulled a pair of binoculars out of his saddlebag and stood up in his stirrups. His horse stood calmly, the reins dropped casually over his neck, while Matt scanned the ridges and slopes.

Kate swung a leg over the mare's neck and hooked it casually in front of the saddle horn.

"Exactly what are we looking for, anyway?" she asked, gazing at Farrell through narrowed eyes.

He'd brought along a rifle, but she had the feeling that he wasn't planning on shooting anything. He was acting more like a ranger studying the lay of the land.

"A reason for the Walkers to be trying to run you off," he replied, focusing the binoculars on a craggy outcropping of rock that followed the creek down a drop of about a hundred feet before the water spilled over a ledge in a thin, icy waterfall. "Tell me, do you own the mineral rights on this property?" he asked.

Kate squinted and shielded her eyes from the glare off the snow. He still wasn't making a great deal of sense to her.

"Yes. Why?"

Farrell lowered the binoculars and sat down in the saddle.

"When I was in Reno I found out that Sam Walker had some rocks sent to a local assayer not too long ago. It was the second time in over a year."

He tucked the binoculars back into his saddlebags while Kate stared at him in growing astonishment as it slowly dawned on her what he was getting at.

"You mean Sam Walker thinks there's gold on this ranch?" she asked in utter amazement and more than a little disbelief.

"Could be," Farrell said noncommittally.

"That's the wildest idea I've heard yet!" Kate scoffed as she swung her leg back over the mare's neck and found the heavy leather and wood stirrup with her toe. "I think the family would have noticed something like that sometime during the past hundred and thirty years, don't you?" she challenged.

Before she could make any more sarcastic rejoinders, however, the words died in her throat, unspoken.

Farrell gave her a quizzical look.

"You look kind of cute with your mouth hanging open," he observed with a grin. "I take it something's occurred to you that makes the idea a little more plausible on second thought?"

Kate glared at him and snapped her jaw shut.

"As a matter of fact, yes," she admitted testily, a little miffed at his ungentlemanly description of her mouth. "It so happens that the first McKendricks did do a little gold mining." She saw Farrell's eyes veritably gleam with triumph and hastened to add, "But they never found anything."

Farrell didn't seem too disturbed at her pronouncement. He merely reined his horse back toward home.

"Well, maybe we'll have more luck," he said. "Come on. Let's get back before it gets dark."

Kate urged the mare back down the mountain.

"If you wanted to get back before dark, we should have left about half an hour ago," she grumbled. "By the way, how did you stumble across a rumor like that in Reno, for heaven's sake?" she asked with a frown.

Farrell grinned at her.

"Sooner or later you hear just about all of them in a Nevada casino," he replied easily.

"And I'm a monkey's uncle!" Kate mumbled crossly. Why in the dickens did the man have to play his cards so close to his vest, for heaven's sake? After all, they were on the same side, she thought irritably. And it was her ranch, for crying out loud!

"If you get any madder, there'll be steam rising off your head," Farrell teased her, still grinning broadly.

"Well try being a little less poker-faced, Farrell," she snapped. "Sometimes it's downright annoying!"

His laughter followed her as she kicked the mare into a lope. Damn but he could be irritating, she thought, trying to ride out her frustration.

CHAPTER SEVEN

Loren McKendrick was not as skeptical as his daughter-in-law.

"Gold, eh?" he said, rubbing the gray stubble on his chin with gnarled fingertips. "Well. It's possible. Back in the 1850s when John McKendrick brought the first Katherine McKendrick here as a bride, he thought there might be some gold up in those hills." McKendrick squinted his eyes thoughtfully. "He even did some digging around, as the story goes. Far as I know, though, he never found any."

Farrell looked at the oil painting hung on the wall facing the fireplace. He'd wondered about the woman portrayed in it. The name engraved on the small brass nameplate attached to the frame had been particularly intriguing. It said, "Katherine Solace McKendrick, beloved wife of John."

"Kate was named after her," Loren remarked in a suspiciously casual drawl. He chuckled and added, "And she's turned out to be just as stubborn and independent as her namesake!"

Before Matt could ask how Kate came to be named after a McKendrick forebear, the contemporary subject of their conversation entered the room.

"I think I've memorized that bedtime story," Kate complained with a laugh. "And I *know* Jason has! If I so much as change one little word he corrects me!"

"Is he asleep?" Loren asked out of habit.

Kate nodded. Putting Jason to bed was one of her favorite activities of the day. He looked so innocent and vulnerable lying there tangled up with his favorite toys and blankets. Once his little eyes closed, he looked like a perfect angel.

Kate sighed contentedly and tried to redirect her thoughts to the problems at hand.

"What do you think about Matt's theory that the Walkers believe we've got a gold mine out there somewhere, Pop?"

"Could be, Katherine Solace," he replied with a sage twinkle in his old eyes. "It just could be."

Farrell took in her slim figure with pleasure. Her yellow cotton shirt showed the wear and tear of wrestling a five-year-old boy through his bath and into bed. Her sleeves were rolled up and the front was spotted with water drops. Her jeans, molding her curves with faithful precision, were damp here and there. Small wisps of light brown hair curled around her face.

The McKendricks had a gold mine, as far as Farrell was concerned. And she was standing just a few feet away from him.

He strode over to the old wooden coat tree next to the front door. He tried to ignore the silence that suddenly fell on the parlor in his wake. He yanked on his heavy fleece-lined leather jacket and pulled his Stetson off its perch.

"It's getting late," he muttered, pulling the Stetson down low over his brow. "I think I'll be going. Night, Loren. Kate."

Kate, too startled by his abrupt exit to think of anything brilliant to say, stood with her mouth half open in surprise.

"Night," said her equally surprised father-in-law. "He sure seemed in a hurry," he added in amusement as the door slammed shut.

Kate didn't feel the cold blast of air that snaked through the parlor. She was numb with confusion and outrage. She had no idea why she should feel so outraged, but she didn't stop to analyze it.

"You'd think he left just because I showed up!" she exclaimed in dismay as a soft shade of coral crept into her cheeks.

Loren looked out the window at Farrell, who could just barely be seen in the darkness. Then the old man's sharp old eyes turned back on his daughter-in-law.

"Maybe you're right," he agreed as a gleam of humor began to light his eyes.

Kate, deaf to the undertone in her father-in-law's voice, stamped her foot and walked stiffly over to the window. She saw Farrell go into the barn.

"If he thinks he can go digging for gold on this ranch without including me in his plans, he'd better think again!" she mut-

116

tered in annoyance. She whirled and eyed Loren critically. "Did he convince you there was gold out there, Pop?"

Loren shook his head and looked as innocent as he could.

"Nope. He didn't try. But then, he didn't have to convince me, Kate."

"Why not?"

"Why, 'cause I already think there probably is."

Kate gave an unladylike snort of disbelief.

Her father-in-law put up a weather-beaten hand to still her doubts.

"They don't call these the mother lode counties for nothin', Kate," he reminded her.

Kate couldn't argue with that.

"Where are *you* going?" her father-in-law asked mildly as Kate stamped over to the coat tree and yanked her heavy coat off it.

"I'm going to make sure the horses are settled for the night," she muttered.

"Oh." The way Loren said it made it sound like he didn't believe a word she said and didn't mind her knowing it.

Kate glared at him and yanked the door open.

"Well why else would I be going out?" she snapped.

Her father-in-law looked at her innocently.

"I wouldn't know."

Kate slammed the door after her and walked toward the barn, where a light still glowed. She was going to talk about this ridiculous theory on gold mines whether Matt Farrell wanted to or not, she fumed. Even if she had to corner the man in the barn with a pitchfork and make him talk to her! She was sick and tired of being avoided like some Typhoid Mary!

She found him bent over in the gray's stall, examining one of the horse's hoofs.

She latched the barn door to keep out the blast of cold air that was following her in.

"Something wrong?" she asked coolly, standing just inside with hands shoved deep into her coat pockets.

He didn't even look up.

"Nope," came the voice from inside the stall.

"Are you still planning on going hunting?" she asked bluntly, walking a little closer.

117

Farrell ran a hand up the horse's leg, feeling for any swelling or tenderness.

"Yeah."

Nope. Yeah. He was a real fountain of information, Kate thought in annoyance.

"Hunting for what, Farrell?" she asked in a slightly louder voice as she reached the door to the stall.

He straightened and looked over the gray horse, running a hand lightly over withers and back.

"For gold."

Kate gritted her teeth and grasped the top of the stall's half door with both hands.

"Where, if you don't mind my asking," she pursued, a definite sarcastic edge to her voice this time, "are you planning on starting the hunt?"

Farrell lifted a large blanket off the wall next to him and eased it onto his horse's back.

"You look all right, pal," he said in a soft voice. "For someone who's been living a soft life, you made out okay."

Kate raised her eyes heavenward in search of divine strength to prevent her losing her temper.

"Farrell! Do you have someplace in particular to start this wild-goose chase or are we just going to wander around the ranch until we fall into a gold mine?" she practically shouted in frustration.

Farrell, still ignoring Kate, walked to the back of the stall and picked up the bridle he'd hung on a hook earlier.

"I have a couple of ideas," he replied as he eased by his horse and lifted the latch to leave the stall.

Kate was standing on the lower slat of the door and staring at him. Matt, forced to look at the woman standing on his stall door, frowned.

"Would you mind?" he asked curtly, indicating with a nod of his head that he wanted her to get off so he could get out.

"Yes, I would mind!" she retorted. "I want you to stay put long enough for us to talk about this!"

Farrell dropped his gaze and pushed open the stall door, with Kate on it.

"So talk," he ordered.

Kate jumped down and latched the door for him as he carried his bridle over to a tree stump in the corner that served as a stool. He sat down, opened a tin of saddle soap, and began cleaning the leather straps with a clean cloth.

"Where are we planning on starting?" she asked, struggling to be more reasonable and sound like a normal human being again.

"Up along that ledge you showed me today," he answered curtly.

"Why do you think that's a good place?" she asked curiously.

"The rock formations are similar to some in other parts of the Sierra that have produced gold," he replied without looking up.

Kate sat down on an ancient stool next to him.

"You sound like you've done some mining before," she said in surprise.

"Some."

"What kind?" She'd drag it out of him one answer at a time if she had to! If that's the way he wanted to do it, it was okay by her, she swore.

"Hard rock. Placer."

"Hm. John McKendrick and you would have gotten along just fine, you know that, Farrell?"

Farrell looked at her and raised an eyebrow in surprise.

"Is that so?" he asked.

Kate grinned impishly and leaned toward him challengingly.

"Yes! He was a seaman who got swept up in the gold craze of the forty-niners. He got himself a pick ax and a pan and went hard-rock mining and placer mining until he made a strike."

That definitely got Farrell's attention.

"He discovered gold?"

"On the other side of the Sierras," Kate qualified. "Then he took his grubstake and the girl he'd fallen in love with and came over here, trying to find another kind of wealth."

Farrell looked perplexed.

"He wanted land?"

Kate shook her head.

"No."

"What then?"

Kate looked into his eyes.

"Family. Home. A place of his own."

Their eyes locked and that strange sizzling whipped through her veins again.

"You think I have something in common with that?" Farrell asked with a bitter laugh. "You're a dreamer, Kate McKendrick!"

She wouldn't back off. Unwavering green eyes dared him to blink first. Farrell abruptly stood up and stalked back to the stall. He hung the bridle on a hook next to the saddle and stared sightlessly at the big gray.

"Some people just aren't cut out for that, Kate," he said distantly.

Farrell rubbed the back of his neck with his hand and tried to think of some way to change the subject. He was drowning in those damned green eyes of hers. Even with his back turned to her!

"Maybe not," she agreed, trying to swallow the hurt his words had dealt her. Why are you letting him get to you? she asked herself crossly.

She walked over to Calamity's stall and the mare nuzzled her hand affectionately.

"Why did you come back?" she asked, her voice barely above a whisper.

It didn't matter. Farrell heard. When Kate spoke he seemed to pick up her voice like a radio receiver.

"T.J.'s still got $50,000 of my money," he reminded her. "I intend to get it back."

She rubbed the mare's velvety black muzzle.

"You weren't planning on coming back until Thanksgiving for that. What happened to make you change your mind?" She heard the slight shake in her voice, but she doubted that Farrell could.

He frowned at her back and began buttoning his heavy jacket.

"I hate to see you lose your land to that overgrown adolescent and his shark of an old man," he said angrily. "Is there something wrong with wanting to help you and your family out?"

Kate whirled.

"No! It's very decent of you!" she practically shouted. She ran forward and caught his arm just before he could open the

120

door. "And stop walking away from me like that! I hate it!" she cried.

They were only inches apart.

He looked down into her eyes, dark with anguish and a maelstrom of conflicting emotions. It was like looking into his soul. She drew him like a mystical force. Before he realized he'd moved, his hands were cupping her head and he was bending toward her. Their lips touched. With a last anguished sigh, Farrell abandoned his resolve to leave her alone. Just one kiss . . . just one sweet moment of delight . . . that was what he intended.

That wasn't what he got.

The velvety warmth of her mouth unlocked the tormented fires within him. He crushed her to him, plundering her mouth with savage intensity, drawing mercilessly from her sweet well.

Kate moaned and leaned into him. When he pulled back she grasped his jacket front to keep from losing her balance.

His lips brushed hers; his warm breath feathered across her skin as he spoke.

"Jesus, Kate," he whispered raggedly. "Don't kiss me back like that!" He closed his eyes and leaned his forehead against hers. "I can't stand it."

Kate felt the gentle rasp of his chin and closed her own eyes.

"Sorry," she whispered unsteadily. "But if you'll recall, you started the kissing, Farrell."

He groaned softly and clenched his jaw.

"Don't remind me," he muttered darkly.

Kate opened her eyes a little and ventured to look up. He was looking at her in the strangest way . . . all open and confused. There was an oddly broken expression in his dark eyes that twisted her heartstrings.

She touched his lips lightly with hers and thrilled as she felt him suck in his breath.

"It's too bad you can't stand kissing me, Farrell," she whispered, her gaze wandering over his face. It was so good to see him this close up, to inhale the unique scent that was his, to watch the pulse beat raggedly in his neck, to tease him unmercifully with a kiss.

"Why?" he asked, caught in her mesmerizing net. He stared

down in rapt fascination, only barely aware of what he was saying.

She looped her arms around his neck.

"Because I kind of liked kissing you," she murmured softly. "So grit your teeth," she said weakly, " 'cause I'm going to do it again."

He saw her face coming closer, but it felt like everything was happening in slow motion. He couldn't seem to move, except to slowly close his eyes in profound pleasure as her gentle lips touched his. He sighed and the breath went from his mouth to hers as her kiss enveloped him in tender wanting. There was only the sensation of her tongue loving his, and then he drew her into his mouth as if he had done it before . . . as if it were right . . . as if it had always been meant to be . . .

Farrell couldn't think anymore, and he'd lost his ability to try. His arms closed around her and he became lost in her spell.

Their mouths fused in exquisite delight and they surrendered themselves into each other's care. It was like falling into an earthquake of desire. The deepening kiss pushed all their repressed needs to the surface in a powerful rush.

Farrell gasped and held her away for a second, struggling to cool the raging fires she'd ignited within him. Kate, drugged with the passion he'd awakened in her, loosened the fastenings of his coat and hers, and slid her arms around him. She sighed with pleasure as she pressed against him. She didn't even mind the layers of clothing that still remained between them. It was such a relief to be rid of the coats and be able to feel the hard, muscled contours of his body.

She snuggled against his neck and reveled in the nearness, pressing kisses against the hot, damp skin of his throat. She was too occupied to notice the spasm of agony that crossed his face, but she heard his groan and hugged him protectively.

Farrell jerked her against him and fiercely kissed her back. She'd nearly broken through every scrap of resistance he had where she was concerned. Fire was coursing through every vein in his body. He ran his hands roughly over her, as if seeking to quench it by touching her. Naturally, it had the opposite effect, and he staggered backward until they collapsed on a pile of fresh straw.

With shaking hands he acquainted himself with the delicious

contours that had tortured his imagination of late. The swell of her breast, the stiff peak that poked proudly up at his tongue, the twisting curve of her hip as he pulled her against him in rhythmic strokes. The more he tried to ease his fires, the higher the flames shot until he turned his face abruptly away from her and held her stiffly at arm's length.

Kate was trembling from head to toe. She'd never felt so much a woman in her entire life. That liquid flame that licked her insides could only be fed by one man. She slowly opened her eyes and gazed at him, seeing him as if for the first time.

"I . . ." she whispered huskily, gazing at him like a woman mesmerized.

The rest of the thought stuck in her throat. She didn't know what to say, really. She wanted to tell him how she felt, how he affected her. The problem was, she didn't know what words to use to describe it. The feelings were all new to her. There weren't words to describe how profoundly he touched her.

Farrell lay rigidly still and looked back in torment. One more touch of her hands or mouth on his body and he was done for. He hadn't felt so hot since he was seventeen. And yet he couldn't bear to let her go from him.

He reached out and gently touched her cheek, tracing her lovely features with new eyes.

He pulled her back into his arms, pressing her head against his chest and telling her to be still. It was pure torture. And pure ecstasy.

A little while later Farrell lay stretched out in the straw, one arm cradling Kate's head, the other pulling her into the warmth of his body. His coat was under them. Hers, over them.

"Katherine Solace," he murmured. "What a misnamed woman you are," he sighed in frustration.

She snuggled up against the warmth of his red plaid shirt and mumbled into his chest.

"Why's that?"

"You're not a solace, you're a torment!" he complained huskily. "Are you ever a torment!"

She ran her palm farther around his waist and pressed the length of her body against him.

"A torment, am I!" she exclaimed, feigning mild outrage. "Then take that."

She felt him flinch as her body imprinted itself against his. When he automatically tightened his arms and sought her neck with his lips, she threw back her head and smiled in pleasure.

"And that," she whispered unevenly as she hugged him tighter still.

Farrell groaned and pulled her on top of him. Every inch of his body was hungry for her. He couldn't get close enough to her with all their clothes still on. A fragile remnant of sanity kept him from tearing them all off and satisfying his desperate need of her.

He kissed her neck, letting his lips slide slowly down from her jaw to her collarbone. At the same time his hands traveled over her back and shoulders in exquisite, leisurely exploration. Sweet torment. Each touch . . . each kiss . . .

Kate curved her arms behind his shoulders and moved sensuously against the long, tough length of him. Even in her passion-drugged awareness, she felt him tense and harden against her. Knowing he was as aroused by her as she was by her made her want to sing with joy. But she was much too busy rubbing her lips teasingly against his cheek to bother with singing!

Farrell moaned hoarsely and buried his face in Kate's neck. He swore incoherently against the soft, warm flesh and clenched his fists behind her back.

"If you don't stop wiggling like that, this isn't going to stop with a little kissing!" he warned in a very hoarse voice. He grabbed her forearms and pushed her firmly off him. "It's going to be a full-fledged roll in the hay."

He jackknifed into a sitting position and dropped his head into his palms, trying to think of poker hands he'd like to have . . . anything to block out the tidal wave of desire that was threatening to overwhelm him.

Kate lay propped up on both elbows.

"That's a terrible pun, Farrell," she laughed unsteadily.

He looked over at her ruefully, then gave the barn a cursory once-over.

"Yeah," he admitted wryly. "Sorry," he sighed.

Kate sat up and straightened her clothing. She'd never had a "roll in the hay," as Farrell had so prosaically put it. Tonight was as close as she'd ever come to it. As she tucked in her shirt and plucked some straw off her clothes, she almost wished he hadn't stopped.

He ran a hand lightly over her long braid of hair, pulling off some straw here and there. There was a clouded look in his eyes. He didn't look like a very happy man to Kate.

"Why the sad look?" Kate asked softly. Then, trying to tease him back into a better humor, she added, "Kissing me wasn't *that* awful, was it?"

Farrell managed a guilty grin and shook his head.

He stood up, pulling Kate to her feet a few seconds later.

"No," he admitted, forcing an unconvincing smile.

He ran his hands through his hair and bent down to put on his jacket. The barn was cold. Without Kate's warm body next to him, he finally realized that.

"I just don't want you to take it the wrong way, Kate," he said.

Kate put on her jacket and tilted her chin in a show of feminine pride.

"How many ways can you take a kiss?" she asked testily. "A kiss is a kiss. Period. People kiss all the time. Ask the kids in the local high school! It's no big deal."

Farrell gritted his teeth and glowered at her.

"That wasn't what I was talking about, and you know it, damn it! That was a hell of a lot more than a kiss! And I'd bet my bottom dollar even the kids in high school around here would have the sense to know that!"

Kate stuffed her hands in her pockets.

"Well, then, what is your point?" she asked challengingly, although it took some courage to do so.

Farrell paced back and forth.

"I'm not here to chase you," he said curtly. "I'm here to help you out and get my money back. And then I'm leaving. So let's not complicate things by getting involved with each other. Okay?"

His "okay" sounded more like an order than a plea for her agreement.

"Well you don't have to make such a big deal out of it, Farrell!" she said crossly. Why did he have to go and spoil that lovely feeling that had enveloped them? she wondered unhappily. "I'm a big girl, remember?"

Farrell was trying very hard *not* to remember that. He frowned and stalked around the barn, trying to walk off a little of the tension.

"Yeah," he muttered darkly.

"So what time do we go hunting for gold tomorrow?" she asked, pleased at how natural her voice sounded. It certainly didn't reflect her feelings at the moment.

"I thought *I'd* leave about an hour before sunup," Farrell said, lowering his eyebrows and voice for added effect. "Alone."

He gave her an intimidating look, which Kate effortlessly ignored.

"Well you'd better think again, then, Farrell! This is *my* ranch. I'm going along," she declared emphatically.

"You showed me how to get there today," he pointed out. "There's no need for you to go along."

"No need?" she echoed, surprised at his choice of words. "For heaven's sake, Matt, it's my land. It has nothing to do with whether I'm needed or not."

Farrell's jaw tightened. He didn't want to spell it out for her, but she was making it difficult not to. He made one last effort to dissuade her without giving her the real reason.

"Don't you have to check on the cattle or do some work around here? Maybe start organizing that ace in the hole of yours next door?" he asked with a wave of one hand toward the wall he'd built for her.

"It can wait," she said succinctly. "See you in a few hours."

She started to walk past him, but he stepped in front of her.

"Your father-in-law was right," he muttered in exasperation. "You are one stubborn woman!" He placed a hand on the door just in case she got any ideas about trying to open it. "I don't want you to go, Kate. Find something else to do tomorrow!"

"Give me one good reason why I shouldn't go," she challenged, green fire smoldering defiantly in her eyes.

"Because it might be dangerous!" he thundered. "If I'm right the Walkers may be keeping an eye on your property, just in case you stumble onto the same thing they have! It wouldn't be the first time someone tried to eliminate the person standing

126

between them and sudden wealth! And so far they haven't seemed too hospitable, if you ask me!"

Kate gaped at him.

"You think they'd attack us?" she asked, truly shocked.

"Not them personally. Hired help."

Kate swallowed hard and remembered the fight at the Johnsons' General Store. And T.J.'s unrelenting efforts to interest her in a relationship of some sort with him.

"I guess it's possible," she conceded reluctantly. She buttoned the top button on her coat. "Is that why you brought the rifle?" she asked bluntly.

Farrell dropped his arm from the door.

"Partly. And also as camouflage. I can always say I'm hunting. Maybe someone'll even believe me. You never know."

Kate didn't want any more conversation. She just wanted to go to sleep and forget about everything for a few hours. She'd grown up with T.J. Although she didn't care for him, it was hard to think that he might intend her any real harm.

Taking her land was bad enough. Threatening to harm her . . . that was pretty hard to comprehend. . . .

"I think I'll turn in," she said faintly.

Farrell, worried at the effect his words might have had, reached out and touched her cheek with the palm of his hand. She was such a gentle-hearted creature, he thought tenderly. He felt a violent surge of anger against the Walkers for what they were putting her through. If T.J. or his father had been present, Farrell would have been sorely tempted to beat each of them senseless. As it was, he was standing here, helpless to get to the root of her problem, not in a position to really champion her cause. That privilege was reserved for the men of her family. Like a father . . . or a husband.

"Forget what I said, Kate," he urged her, his low voice steeped in concern. He grinned self-deprecatingly. "I always plan for the worst. No matter how unlikely."

Kate's eyelids fluttered, and for a moment she was hidden from his scrutiny. How dearly she wished that everything would just melt away! She rested her cheek against his comforting palm and tried to push away the despair that tugged at her.

She nodded her head slightly and caught his hand with hers.

"Sure, Matt. Whatever you say." She felt so tired of it all. She was beginning to wonder whether it was worth it. After all, it was just land. She pressed her cheek against his palm and pulled away.

"Night, Matt."

He watched her go, wishing he could be with her, wanting to comfort her, to ease the discouragement for her. An hour later, stretched out on the hide-a-bed couch in the old homestead, he was still seeing her, still wishing he was with her, still missing her so.

"I thought I told you I was going alone!"

Farrell had just come into the barn. Finding Kate saddling up her mare was not getting the day off to a good start, as far as he was concerned.

"You did."

"But you're going anyway?"

"Right."

Farrell stamped angrily around the stall, muttering impolite observations about Kate's powers of deductive reasoning while saddling the big gray horse in record time.

He walked the animal outside. It was still dark. The cold morning air chilled them to the bone. He swung up into the saddle in one easy motion, then dug in his heels. He pulled down his Stetson as the horse leaped forward.

"It's your nickel," he said, distancing himself from any responsibility in the event of a disaster.

"Exactly," she muttered under her breath.

Farrell hadn't noticed the rifle that Kate had tucked in her own gear. He'd been too irritated to see much of anything after he'd caught sight of her.

Kate swung up into the saddle and urged the mare forward. As Calamity broke into an easy lope Kate whistled. A black streak tore past her.

"At least there'll be one friend on this trip," Kate reassured herself. She grimaced and made a face at Farrell's back. "One friend and one dog in the manger," she griped, relaxing in the saddle as the mare found an easy stride and relentlessly ate up the ground ahead of them.

Farrell's anger mellowed into disgruntled frustration. By the time they reached the ledge, he was resigned to Kate's company. He pulled the big gray horse to a halt and stood up in the stirrups to stretch his legs.

"Not used to riding?" Kate asked in a suspiciously mild voice.

Farrell turned his head and looked at her for the first time since they'd left the ranch.

"Not recently," he admitted in a cool, distant voice.

Kate cocked her head to one side and looked at him curiously.

"How did you learn, anyway?" she asked with her customary bluntness. "You ride like a cowboy," she observed.

Farrell grinned faintly.

"You don't have to sound so surprised," he retorted.

Kate shrugged.

"So . . . have you done some cowboying, Farrell?" she persisted.

"Yeah. When I was a teenager. On the ranches where my mother worked." He sat down slowly. The leather creaked softly at the shifting weight. "A couple of the owners were pretty decent fellows. They taught me . . . took me on in spite of everything."

Kate heard the mixture of respect and humiliation that still lingered in his recollection of those long-ago events. She urged the mare forward a few steps until her horse was shoulder to shoulder with Farrell's horse.

"A lot of us have been where you were, Farrell," she said softly.

Farrell gave her a skeptical look.

"It's true!" she exclaimed. "Why most of the families that settled around here back in the old days had some pretty shady characters in them . . . gunfighters, saloon girls, people looking for something for nothing, land speculators . . ."

Farrell grinned at her.

"Sounds like things haven't changed much," he observed.

Kate smiled back.

"I guess not."

They both looked away. The intimacy came back in a rush when they looked at each other for very long.

Farrell shifted uncomfortably in the saddle and made a losing effort at shaking off a violent surge of desire. He wanted to pull

129

her off the mare, drag her into the pine-scented forest, and lie down with her until neither of them wanted to think ever again.

He grimaced and shielded his eyes, though it wasn't sunlight that had marred his expression. It was frustration . . . and anguish . . . and wanting something he kept telling himself he absolutely *could not* have. And yet, he wanted her so . . .

Kate made a show of checking the cheek strap on the mare, but she really just needed an excuse to bend forward and hide her face from Farrell for a moment. She was sure if he saw it, he'd see how much she was longing for him. He was obviously not interested in pursuing their relationship, such as it was. He certainly wouldn't appreciate having her lay her heart on her sleeve for him to feel sorry for!

She bit her lip and tried to get a hold on her unhappy thoughts.

Stiffly, they looked back at each other. Neither one was quite sure what to do with their feelings. Neither had much luck coming up with anything to say to help smooth over the awkward moment, either.

"I'm going down and take a closer look," Farrell announced abruptly. He dismounted and handed Kate his horse's reins.

"Why don't you figure out something to do with the horses," he suggested as he removed a pickax from a bundle tied behind his saddle.

"Why not?" Kate muttered in annoyance as he disappeared over the steep drop down to the ledge.

She tied the horses to a rope and tethered them to a tree, still trembling from the impact of looking at Farrell. That wonderful thrill of awareness and desire . . . a heartwarming touch of caring and wanting . . . all mixed together into a feeling so unique, so new, that she couldn't put a name to it.

"Well, maybe I *can* put a name to it," she murmured as she stroked Calamity's neck. "But I don't want to. I sure don't want to," she sighed unhappily.

Kate shook her head to clear it of the melancholy that threatened. She hung over the edge to look down on Farrell.

"How're you making out?" she called out to him.

Farrell took another swing at the rock. Pieces flew apart, cascading in a small shower down the ledge into the half-frozen creek. He leaned the pick against his thigh and flexed his gloved hands.

"Digging through frozen rock's great fun!" he answered sarcastically. "Other than that, I've got nothing to report."

Kate watched him examine some of the newly exposed rock. It looked like it would be a long morning to her.

"Anything I can do to help?" she asked seriously.

Farrell shook his head.

"Just make sure the horses don't head for home without me," he replied with real warning.

Kate smiled down at him and gave herself over to the pleasure of watching him swing a pickax.

"Right, Farrell."

Doc, who'd scoured the woods for interesting scents, came back and sat down beside Kate.

"Guess we'll just have to hurry up and wait, Doc," Kate teased the big furry animal as she gave his ears a friendly scratch.

They were both getting pretty bored of doing nothing when relief came from an unexpected quarter.

Doc growled and twisted around with a jerk just as Kate noticed a glint of light high in the trees on a neighboring slope. The dog's ears, like the rest of him, had snapped to attention.

"What is it, Doc?" Kate murmured, squinting to try and make out the source of the reflection.

The crack of a rifle shot answered her question.

Farrell swore as the bullet struck rock nearby and slivers exploded in all directions. He scrambled up the rocky drop and rolled over the edge.

Kate was already gone.

"What in the hell?" he exclaimed as another shot rang out. This one from near the horses.

He twisted in time to see Kate lower a rifle from her shoulder.

The bright pinpoint of light disappeared, along with a small blur of dark red.

"It could have been a hunter," Kate said slowly. "I fired into the treetops, just to let him know we were here. He left."

Farrell dusted the snow off his clothes and gave her an incredulous look.

"Sure," he said agreeably, although there was a definite note of sarcasm behind his even words. "Anything is possible. I'd say the odds are increasingly in your favor, though."

"The odds that there's gold on the ranch?"

"Yes."

Kate shoved the rifle back into the boot.

"It's not worth getting shot for," she said stubbornly. "Why don't we call it quits, Farrell? There's got to be another way to go about this. A way that doesn't involve getting used for target practice."

Farrell had been only two feet from the bullet's path. Under the circumstances he thought Kate had a good point.

The horses were snorting and milling and tugging at the tether, but they were right where Kate had left them. Farrell helped her untie them.

"There's more than one way to put an end to that problem," he said in a hard voice. He slipped a toe into the stirrup and mounted the gray. He gave a last, searching look in the direction from which the shot had come. "I think we'd better go straight to the source."

CHAPTER EIGHT

It was a long ride back. It seemed even longer because of the strained silence that hung between Kate and Farrell. Kate was determined to call the sheriff and report the shooting incident, just to be on the safe side. Farrell had laughed cynically when she told him that. He had told her it would just be a waste of her time. Kate had angrily bet him he'd be proved wrong.

As he watched her hang the receiver back on the hook later that afternoon, he knew he'd been proved right instead. It didn't make him feel particularly triumphant, however. Far from it. He was left feeling hollow and angry for her sake. He hated to see Kate's faith in her longtime friend crumble into disillusionment.

Farrell knew the taste of disillusionment. He didn't wish it on her.

"Is he going to do anything about it?" Farrell asked gently.

Kate lifted her shoulders and shook her head slightly.

"Well . . . he said he'd ride out there tomorrow and see if he could find some tracks or marks that would help identify the rifleman. If it looks like it was just some hunter, he'll drop it at that." Kate took a deep breath and sighed. "If it looks questionable, he said he'd try to dig around and find out what's going on."

It was the way Vern had said it that upset her. She doubted that he would be willing to make a case out of it unless it was so obvious that a blind man could see it!

Kate walked into the parlor and dropped into a chair.

"That's more than I thought he'd be willing to do, Kate," Farrell offered. And indeed it was. Maybe Vern Peterson possessed a cautious streak of independence in spite of his obvious desire not to make waves.

Farrell put on his coat and walked toward the door. Doc sat up and followed along, hanging uncertainly on three paws when Farrell opened the door.

Farrell leaned down and gave the big black animal a casual pat on the head.

Doc laid his ears back but accepted the contact politely.

Kate was astonished.

"I think I'll go check on the horses," Farrell said. Anything to keep his mind from where it kept wandering, he told himself as he stepped into the cold. It was almost as good as a cold shower, he thought in cynical amusement.

Kate pointed a slender finger at Doc.

"That's the first time I've ever seen you let a stranger touch you!" she exclaimed.

Doc lowered his head onto the hand-sewn coil-shaped rug in front of the door. His ears flattened out to the sides, making him look a little abashed.

Kate smiled and began to laugh softly.

"It's all right, Doc. I know how you feel," she murmured. "I know just how you feel."

Kate curled her feet under her and leaned back in the old overstuffed wing chair. She listened to the floorboards creak as Loren walked from the bathroom into his bedroom. Soon the soft crackle of the dying fire was her only company. Even Doc went to sleep.

Try as she might, sleep would not come to Kate, however. The face of an enigmatic gambler kept haunting her. She opened her eyes and turned to look out the window. The light in the old homestead still burned.

"If you weren't going to sleep, Farrell, you could have stayed here and kept me company," she said softly.

Kate grabbed her coat and quietly left the house. If the mountain wouldn't come to Muhammad, Muhammad would just have to go to it, she told herself.

"It sure would help if Muhammad's knees would just stop knocking," she muttered under her breath a few minutes later as she prepared to knock on the cabin door.

Farrell answered on the first knock. The door swung open fast and he looked out in obvious surprise.

"Is something wrong?" he asked sharply.

134

Kate took the opportunity to duck inside and shed her coat.

"No," she hedged. "I saw your light, and, since you were still up, and I was still up, well, there were a few things we never quite wrapped up this afternoon." She marched over to the potbellied stove and warmed her hands as if it were the most natural thing in the world for her to do.

The door closed.

Farrell ran a hand around the waist of his jeans, tucking in loose edges of his shirt here and there.

"Like what?" he inquired blankly. He'd been stunned to see her standing outside his door. Having her waltz into the small cabin that served as his bedroom wasn't helping to restore his equilibrium.

Kate's glance ricocheted off Farrell and flew quickly around the room.

"Like what we should do next," she said, although she'd had to mentally rehearse the "we" a few times before she could actually say it.

Farrell, nonplussed, stared at her in obvious surprise.

"About searching for gold," Kate hastily explained, blushing as she realized her statement could have been taken in a much more personal way.

Farrell ran a finger around his collar and breathed a sigh of relief. He had instantly pictured a number of things that they could do next, but he couldn't believe Kate had any of them in mind when she'd asked her question.

He stalked to the opposite end of the small room and stood facing her somberly.

"What about it?" he prompted her.

"If there is gold on the ranch, is there some way of finding out without spending a fortune digging around looking for it first?" she asked, pouring herself a cup of coffee from the old metal pot warming on top of the stove.

"Probably not," he replied carefully. "I'm not a mining engineer or a geologist, so I could be dead wrong," he reminded her. "As far as I know you have to spend the time doing the looking yourself, or pay someone who's an expert to look for you. Experts usually like to bring along their favorite equipment." He shrugged philosophically and concluded, "Expert time and modern equipment don't usually come cheap. Doing it yourself, on the other hand, can take a lifetime."

Kate swallowed the coffee and choked.

"Good lord, Farrell! How long's this coffee been keeping warm?" she gasped.

He grinned ruefully and shook his head.

"Quite a while, I'm afraid."

Kate dumped the awful-tasting stuff down the drain in the small kitchen area in the back, thumping cans and tins in her search for the bag of coffee and fresh water.

"Hey, don't make any more. I don't need any more!" he called out to her testily.

Kate marched back into the main room and metal slapped softly against metal as the ready-to-brew coffeepot returned to the burner.

Farrell ran a hand through his hair. Kate looked like she was settling in for a long talk. Just what I need, he thought in frustration. A nice long talk in the middle of the night all alone in a cabin with Kate. He stuffed his hands into the back pockets of his jeans and stared blankly at her. Maybe he could still find enough self-discipline to pretend that his palms weren't beginning to sweat and his skin to tingle at her presence. And the soft, fragrant scent of her wasn't bothering him at all either, he vaguely tried to convince himself.

"You said something about going straight to the source earlier," she reminded him, nervously plucking at the quilt folded over the back of the couch now that she had no coffee cup to hang on to. "What did you mean by that?"

Farrell had to concentrate to follow her train of conversation. It was annoying that she could be so calm and collected about it, he thought. He was gritting his teeth to keep from looking like an adolescent fool and there she was rattling on about some rational, thinking activity!

"I don't have a grand plan, if that's what you're asking," he answered curtly. "It just seemed to me that it would make more sense to tackle Sam Walker and his son directly. Eliminate their interest in your land somehow. Then go look for mineral deposits. That way you'd have a chance to do your prospecting without getting shot in the back in the process."

"That makes sense." There was an awkward silence. Kate

tried to think of something to follow up his idea, to keep him talking. His voice was soothing and reassuring to her, even though he was not looking too pleased at having her invade his privacy.

Unfortunately, Kate had run out of excuses. And seeing him staring at her so coolly, with that subtle air of distrust clinging to him, was the last straw.

She picked up her coat and walked stiffly toward the door.

"Well . . . thanks for the coffee. Sorry to bother you. I can see you'd rather be alone."

She didn't look at him. She couldn't. The only way she could get out of that cabin without showing more than she wanted was to keep her eyes off him. She watched her hand close over the doorknob as she prepared to open the door and leave.

Her voice fell to a strained whisper.

"I'll see you tomorrow," she forced herself to say.

The fine thread of pain in her rich, sweet voice sliced through his defenses more effectively than anything else ever could have.

Before she could pull the door open, he'd closed the chasm between them and closed his hand over hers.

"Why did you come here, Kate?" he asked hesitantly, afraid to ask yet needing to know the answer, no matter how much it might hurt.

Kate swallowed and stared down at his hand over hers.

"I just wanted to talk to you," she said in a soft, unsteady voice that twisted Farrell's heart.

Farrell saw the pulse beating in her throat and felt a surge of very primitive, very masculine triumph flood through his veins in spite of himself. Maybe she wasn't as unaffected as she'd tried to appear, he thought. And maybe those kisses the other night that had been driving him crazy in his dreams had bothered her some too.

He slid his hand up her wrist and arm, coming to rest just under her chin.

"Why aren't you looking at me?" he asked softly.

Kate felt him pull her face up toward him and she fiercely closed her eyes.

"Because I don't want you to know why I really came out here tonight," she admitted, the words sounding as if they'd been wrenched from her against her will.

137

He moved his hand to cup her cheek and bent to kiss her lightly on the lips. Her eyes opened slowly. He was staring down at her, a naked look in the depths of his eyes.

"I just wanted to be with you," she whispered. "I like being with you," she added, touching his cheek tenderly with her fingertips.

A sharp stab of desire flashed through Farrell, starting at the point where her fingers brushed his cheek and ending in his belly. He sucked in his breath and closed his eyes, turning away and pacing across the room in one last-ditch effort to keep from doing something irreversible.

"And I like being with you, Kate McKendrick," he muttered. He bit his lower lip until the pain got to him. "I like you enough not to want you hurt, or disappointed, or disillusioned. I like you enough to want to leave you alone."

He glanced over his shoulder and gave her a telling look.

"And you and I both know that if we have many more of these late-night 'conversations' they're going to be conducted in a very intimate form of body language!"

He tried to sound harsh and crude, trying to shake her up a little.

Kate's eyes widened in surprise. Then she moved toward him slowly.

"Are you trying to scare me off, Matt Farrell?" she asked challengingly.

"Yes! That's exactly what I'm trying to do, damn it!" he snapped.

Maybe if he could convince himself he was angry with her he could cool down the flames of desire that were burning hotter and hotter with every step she took toward him.

Kate stopped an arm's length away.

"Don't you think I'm old enough to know what I'm doing?" she challenged. "I like *you*, Matt, not your accoutrements . . . not your friends . . . not your social connections. . . ." She stared defiantly at him, her feelings showing in her eyes in spite of her vow to keep them hidden. "What's wrong with that? Why can't we be friends?" she demanded hotly.

Farrell reached out and pulled her roughly into his arms.

"This is why," he muttered just before his mouth came down hard on hers.

Kate felt the frustration and desire burning in him as his lips seared hers like hot coals. He ground his mouth against hers until her lips parted for him. As his tongue touched her mouth something changed. Kate felt the anguish behind his passion and reached out to draw him nearer.

"Kate, Kate," he murmured, kissing her cheeks and eyes and holding her head cradled in his hands. "We can't be friends," he said in a strangled voice as his mouth closed over hers again in a hungry kiss.

He slid his hands down the jacket front, freeing buttons urgently. He thrust his hands inside and pulled her close to his chest, flattening her against him, pressing her close with a hand at her back.

Kate closed her eyes and leaned into his hard, tense body, delirious with the sensations his touch aroused in her, wanting only more.

He gave her shirt a rough tug upward, freeing the fabric from her jeans and giving him access to her bare stomach. The warmth of his palm seared a path of exquisite pleasure from her waist to her breast. His fingers closed over the gentle swell of her flesh. Kate heard his half-swallowed sigh of pleasure and felt a thrill of triumph that he should want her so.

"Ah, Katie, you are a torment," he complained mournfully as he pressed her head into his shoulder and closed his eyes in agony. "You are everything I've ever wanted in a woman," he whispered raggedly, grimacing from the effort to quell his raging need for her.

He dug his fingers into her, not realizing the pain he caused. Kate caught her breath just as he relaxed the pressure.

"I'm not your kind," he argued harshly, a bitter expression clouding his handsome features. "You'd better go home while you still can, Katherine Solace . . ." he murmured in an anguished sigh.

He opened his eyes and looked down at her.

Kate cupped his face in her gentle hands and gazed into his passion-darkened eyes.

"And if I don't?" she asked in tender longing.

Farrell stopped breathing, telling himself not to believe the message she was sending him. It couldn't be. It had to be some twisted trick of his own mind. He wanted her so much. . . .

139

He shut his eyes and straightened his shoulders, bracing himself with the last of his strength to let her go.

"You know what will happen if you don't go, Kate," he muttered thickly. "Leave. Go. Please," he pleaded, his voice showing the strain.

Kate shrugged the jacket from her shoulders, still standing toe to toe with him. He heard the jacket fall and his eyes snapped open. Kate circled his neck with her arms and stood on tiptoe, slowly leaning into him until her lips were just a breath away from his.

"I know," she said softly as she brushed her lips provocatively across his. She gazed at him through half-closed eyes in the come-hither, catch-me-if-you-can way in which females have looked at their intended quarry for thousands of years. "I can't go any more than you can let me," she said huskily. "And if you don't kiss me again, Matt Farrell, I'm going to go crazy."

He groaned in surrender and lowered his lips the fraction of an inch to hers. This time there was warmth and tenderness where before there had been anger and frustration. Farrell couldn't hang on to his resolve any longer. His feelings for her buried it in an avalanche of longing.

He bent down and swung her up into his arms, not breaking the kiss, and carried her to the couch.

"Are you sure?" he murmured gently, trailing warm, tender kisses down the side of her neck and nuzzling her shirt apart to expose her tender flesh to his gaze.

Kate half closed her eyes, swimming in happiness for the first time in many, many years.

"Yes," she whispered. "I'm sure."

He opened the couch into a bed and slowly undressed her, prolonging the pleasure of seeing her for the first time, kissing her body as the clothing was removed.

Kate felt worshiped and ravished all at the same time. His absorption in knowing her freed her from the remnants of her own shyness and let her remove his clothing as he took hers.

They were two golden people in the flickering lamplight a short time later. Golden people bathed in a golden fire.

Farrell pulled Kate down onto the bed with him, half sighing, half groaning with the pleasure of touching her. The soft curves of her body melted against him. The sweet scent of her skin filled his every breath. Aphrodisiacs for a man who needed none where she was concerned. He tortured himself with the delights of running his hands slowly over the slopes and valleys of her body, lost in a mind-stunning desire for this one woman.

He pressed upward against her. Kate felt what he intended her to feel and blushed in spite of her own overwhelming desire for him.

"I don't want you to get pregnant, Kate," he murmured, whispering into her ear.

"It's all right," she assured him, raising herself on her elbows to look down into his eyes.

For the first time, Kate saw into his soul. No remnant of the armor was in place. The poker face had disintegrated into ashes. He cared for her. He wanted her. He needed her. Kate's heart leaped with joy and she smiled down at him.

I love you, she said silently.

He saw it in her eyes and let himself pretend it was true. Just for tonight he would pretend she was his . . . that she loved him . . . that he loved her. . . .

He turned her gently onto her back and slid into her soft warmth.

"Ah, Katherine Solace," he breathed against her cheek as he nuzzled her, ". . . my love . . ."

They loved each other tenderly, eagerly. Flesh cleaved to flesh, as had been intended from the beginning. The agony and fire of desire fused until they were consumed in its convulsive flames. And the peace of lying together afterward was as sweet as the passion of loving each other had been just moments before.

Farrell rolled onto his back, taking Kate with him. Their mouths blended in a long, sweet kiss as he pulled the quilt up over her back to cover them. Kate curled on top of him, exhausted.

"I told you we couldn't be friends," he murmured tenderly, brushing a damp tendril of hair away from her cheek.

"Mmm," Kate mumbled against his hair-roughened chest. "I think I can take it, Farrell." She ran a hand lovingly over his ribs. "Not being friends has certain compensations," she pointed out drowsily.

He grinned and began to laugh. The rumble in his chest sounded so appealing, she burrowed closer.

He gave her bare bottom a light, affectionate smack.

"You're right about that," he agreed.

They lay together, reluctant to break the closeness that enveloped them, wishing the magic could somehow go on forever . . . that the world that had receded from their awareness would stay gone indefinitely . . . and knowing deep in their hearts that it would not.

Farrell tucked her head under his chin and looped his arms around her.

"When I was a kid I used to dream of a place like this," he said softly. He didn't have to look around the room to see it. The well-oiled wood and homemade linens were filed away, safe in his memory, there to savor and treasure whenever he wanted.

"Hand-sewn quilts and rugs . . . an old stove with the coffee always hot . . . a beautiful woman all my own . . ." He placed a tender kiss on Kate's head. "This is like being given a slice of heaven," he told her.

Kate snuggled against him and wriggled her hands behind his back, hugging him as tightly as she could.

"Thank you," he murmured seriously.

Kate lifted her head and looked down at him in wonder.

"You're welcome," she whispered, thinking that he had given as much to her but not knowing how to put it into words. "And thank you."

He laughed softly and gave her another hug.

"I don't know what for, but whatever it is, you're more than welcome, believe me!"

They both laughed and kissed and stretched languidly.

"Matt," she asked tentatively, leaning on her elbows and looking down at him. "Hasn't there ever been anyone?" she inquired, awkwardly searching for the words. "I mean . . . a girl . . . someone serious?"

He gave her a sad, crooked grin.

"No. The ones I wanted when I was a kid weren't interested in a dirt-poor kid like me. One girl . . . in my senior year in high school . . . was fascinated by the risk in getting involved with a boy from the other side of the tracks." He laughed but the scars of bitterness were still there for Kate to see. "Her father made it clear that he didn't want her playing around with me," he said ruefully.

He took Kate's hand and ran it along a hard ridge that cut diagonally across his back. She turned him partly on his side and saw the old, jagged scars.

"He whipped you?" she cried incredulously.

Farrell, feeling bereft of her, pulled her back against him.

"Yeah. With a strand of barbed wire."

Kate felt the tears well up in her eyes and she laid her cheek against his well-muscled chest. She knew he hadn't said it to get her pity, and she tried hard to swallow the sorrow and pain she felt for him. He felt a tear trickle across his chest and lifted her face to kiss the moisture away.

"Hey," he exclaimed apologetically, "it was years ago. Forget it."

She sobbed and kissed his eyes and mouth until they were both trembling.

"I can't help it," she said brokenly. "I wish it had been me. I wouldn't have let them hurt you like that," she cried fiercely.

Farrell ran his hands up her back and sighed in remorse at having told her and in pleasure at her reaction. He couldn't remember many people ever giving a damn about him over the years. It was still hard for him to believe that Kate did.

"And then later the women were interested only in what they could get from me." He shrugged, then grinned rakishly and tugged playfully at her long braid. "I learned to suffer through that," he said, feigning a stoic attitude.

Kate punched him lightly in the midriff and soon they found themselves wrestling under the covers, laughing and groping and protesting foul plays until Kate finally called for quarter.

"Enough!" she gasped. "I can't catch my breath!"

They were sprawled together in a tangle of quilt and sheets, legs entwined.

Kate looked reluctantly at the small alarm clock on the end table next to the couch.

"I'd better be going," she said softly, running her fingers through his tousled hair. She gave him a quick kiss on the mouth and, with a little untangling, managed to get out of the bed.

Farrell lay on his back, hands laced behind his head, watch-

143

ing her dress. She rebraided her hair and splashed cool water on her face. She still looked well kissed, he thought. Her lips were a little swollen and pink. Her eyes had that deep, luminous look of a satisfied woman. Her skin was the color of a ripe peach, blushing all over from being loved by her man.

He snapped out of bed and pulled on his pants in silence. It was hard letting her go now, he realized. Even harder than it had been before in a way. His body was more at ease this time; but his soul ached even more than it had before for her to stay.

Kate found her coat and walked slowly to the door. He helped her put it on, his hands lingering on the top button.

He kissed her, his lips plying hers with the warm promise she wanted to hear. The promise that he cared for her. That it had meant something to him.

"Kate," he murmured, savoring the sound of her name, his dark eyes troubled. "Are you going to be all right?"

She smiled reassuringly and gave him a last, swift hug.

"Yes. Are you?" she added teasingly, her warm heart shining in her eyes.

He sighed and bent his head against hers lightly. Then he drew himself up and gave her that half smile that so twisted her heart.

"Oh, yeah," he said evenly. "Good night, Kate."

He kissed her.

She left without looking back. It was easier that way.

Loren noticed the change between them at breakfast the next day. It was the way they looked at each other when they thought the other wouldn't notice . . . the way Kate kept coming to stand close to Farrell, going out of her way to serve him personally . . . the strange light in Farrell's eyes when he watched her go into the kitchen . . . the way Kate laughed with a lightheartedness Loren hadn't heard in years.

He noticed. And he was glad for them.

"I think I'll take Jason down to the creek for a walk this mornin'," the elder McKendrick announced gruffly as he helped clean up the dishes a little later.

"Okay, Pop," Kate said, surprised.

Farrell joined Kate at the sink and offered to dry. She cheerfully handed him a dish towel and began attacking the dishes.

Loren herded Jason toward his coat. A few minutes later Kate and Farrell were alone.

"I've been thinking about Sam Walker," Farrell said.

"Anything printable?" Kate inquired dubiously.

Farrell chuckled and stacked the dish he'd been drying on top of the previous one.

"Some of it," he replied. "I've been wondering why he's going to such lengths to get your land. Even if it does turn out to have gold on it, there *are* more conventional approaches," he pointed out. "And if it just has a stray nugget or none at all"—Farrell's brows drew together, perplexed—"he'll have wasted a lot of time and energy, to say nothing of garnering a lot of bad will, for precious little."

Kate handed him the last glass and drained the sink.

"You think he must be under some sort of pressure financially?" Kate asked in surprise.

Farrell nodded.

"It could be. If you don't mind I'd like to call Amos and ask him to talk to a couple of banker friends of ours and see if they know anything about Walker's business circumstances."

Kate looked as astonished as she was feeling at the moment.

"Good heavens, Matt! Everyone in Still Waters thinks of him as the man with the Midas touch . . . everything he becomes involved in reaps profits for him. There's never been even a hint of money problems."

Farrell didn't look worried.

"Next to poker players, bankers are some of the biggest gamblers I know of," he remarked casually. "Unlike professional gamblers, however, bankers bet other people's money and prefer the riskiest odds for their biggest bets."

Kate thought about that for a minute.

"I see your point. If you're a little guy needing a little loan for something local, it's hard as the devil to convince them to chance the money. On the other hand, if you're a big company or a country, the sky's the limit on your line of credit. . . ."

Farrell nodded.

"More or less. What does his bank put out money for around here?" he asked curiously.

"Homes. Ranch and farm loans. Some development projects."

Farrell stared at the wall and nodded absently.

"Hmmm," he muttered, heading toward the phone. "Let's see what Amos can find out for us."

When Farrell hung up the phone a little while later, he found Kate dressed for work.

"Would you be interested in taking a look at my cattle?" she asked, almost shyly. "As a guest, of course, you're free to do as you please," she hurried to add, nervously fingering the leather quirt in her hand. "But I have to go out and check on them, and, well, if you'd care to go along . . . you'd be more than welcome."

She tilted her chin up and tried to pretend it wouldn't matter whether he said yes or no.

Farrell traced her lips with the tip of his finger and looked down at her in amusement.

"You don't really think I'd say no, do you?" he asked softly.

Kate smiled, grabbed his coat and threw it to him.

"Well, a girl never knows!" she exclaimed happily. "Come on then! Get a move on, cowboy! I want to see if you know one end of a steer from the other!"

He grabbed her by the shoulders and whirled her around before she could dash outside.

"There's just one thing I have to take care of first," he murmured, lowering his head to hers.

"I thought you'd never think of it," Kate sighed as his lips touched hers.

And then she was lost in the warmth of his kiss and didn't think about anything at all.

Amos was surprised at how quickly he stumbled onto an answer to Matt's inquiry. As it turned out, their banker in Reno had recently returned from a bankers' conference in Los Angeles. It was the same one that Samuel Walker had attended. And Sam Walker had provided an interesting morsel for the closed-door gossips to chew on. An interesting morsel indeed.

"I don't see why you can't stay here a little while longer, honey," purred Sissy Wells as she watched T.J. climb out of her bed and pull on his pants. "It's only the middle of the afternoon, T.J.!" she pouted, twirling a strand of hair with her finger. She kicked off the sheet and struck a provocative pose.

T.J. laughed and shook his head.

"That won't work now, Sis. Three times an afternoon is my limit. You'll just have to burn until tomorrow, she-cat."

Sissy grimaced and swung her slim legs over the edge of the bed. She pulled on an old silk kimono and watched T.J. tighten his belt.

"Did I help the other day, T.J.?" she asked curiously. "I mean with Kate . . . you never told me." She sashayed up to the big man and pressed herself against him flagrantly. "Did I do good, honey?" she asked huskily.

T.J. shook his head. She never got enough of it, he thought. Usually that suited him fine. It turned him on to have a hot little number like Sissy scratching for him. Right now, however, he'd had enough and it was becoming irritating. The scarcely veiled sexual come-ons were becoming a pain in the neck, among other places.

He removed her arms from around his neck and reached for his coat.

"Yeah. You did just fine."

Sissy put her hands on her hips and looked up at him petulantly.

"We've been seeing each other for a long time now, T.J. I'm not getting any younger, and neither are you," she pointed out. "When are you going to tell your old man about me? When are we getting married?"

T.J. hated it when she started up on that. She'd never mentioned marriage at first. She'd been as happy to have him in the sack as he was to be there. But recently she'd been talking up rings and weddings . . . like most women, he thought, despising the sex and their penchant for the ties that bind.

"Not yet, Sissy," he said angrily. "I told you to stop bringing that up! I'm not ready to get into the traces yet. You know that."

"You get into plenty of other things," she cried nastily, pounding his chest with her fist. "What's the matter, T.J.? Aren't I good enough for your old man?" Her eyes narrowed dangerously. "Aren't I good enough for you?"

She raked her nails down his neck, leaving red marks as her brand on him.

T.J. jerked her wrist back and twisted her over his arm.

"You little she-cat!" he swore angrily. He twisted her arm back until she cried out in pain. "Just don't forget who's wearing the pants around here, Sissy," he warned her.

He gave her a hard look and released her. Sissy looked at him defiantly, rubbing her sore wrist and standing her ground.

"I'll see you day after tomorrow. After dinner," he said curtly. He pulled on his hat and opened the door.

As he slammed the door shut Sissy spat every nasty word she could think of at his retreating back. Then she crumpled onto her disheveled bed and cried her eyes out.

"Damn you, T.J.!" she sobbed. "Damn you!"

Kate's hand swept an arc in the air that reached from the foothills well down into the valley below them.

"This is where I'm wintering the cattle. It's a little more sheltered than the pastureland closer to the house, and it's far enough down from the mountains to avoid some of the animals that wander through looking for a free meal from time to time."

"Like what?" Farrell asked, squinting and shielding his eyes against the sunlight reflecting from the snow.

"Oh, mountain lions . . . bears . . . there aren't many anymore, but we still get some every once in a while," she said.

He gave her a quizzical look.

"You don't sound too bothered by it," he observed in amusement.

Kate gave him a dead level look and a charming grin.

"Nope. I'm a crack shot," she said.

Kate gently laid the reins along one side of the mare's neck and leaned forward slightly. Instantly the horse turned and started down the valley.

"You're modest too!" he chuckled as he followed suit with the gray.

Kate shook her head coltishly and inhaled the fresh, cool air, sitting relaxed and at peace with the world as the mare surged forward in easy strides.

"That too, Farrell!" she laughed. "That too!"

CHAPTER NINE

". . . and then I ran down and hid in the grassy part, Mom. You know . . . where the water didn't come this summer . . . and Grandpa couldn't find me!"

Kate poured a last cup of coffee for the three adults at the dinner table and reached for Jason's glass.

"Do you want some more milk, Jason?" she asked automatically, without looking at him.

His face crumbled into disappointment.

"You're not listening!" he wailed anxiously.

Kate stopped what she was doing and looked at her young son. She had to admit it was a legitimate complaint. She ran the back of her hand across her forehead and went around the table to him.

"I'm sorry, honey," she said, giving his soft cheek a kiss. "I wasn't. If you tell me again I'll try to do better. Okay?" she asked encouragingly.

Jason knew the whip hand when he had it. He gave her a long, measuring look.

"Well, okay," he reluctantly agreed, as if making a great exception in this one case.

He repeated the tale of the afternoon's adventures to his now closely attentive mother.

Loren and Matt went into the parlor and set up the checkerboard. Doc padded softly after them, curling behind the gambler's chair.

"Looks like you've made a friend," Loren noted.

Farrell reached into his pocket, pulled out some beef jerky, and dropped it. Big, black jaws snapped it up before it hit the rug.

"Everybody's got their price, I guess," Matt said, giving the dog a rueful smile.

Loren studied the board, wondering if it was possible to come up with a new first move after so many years of playing this blasted game.

"Maybe," he granted. "But you're the first person I've ever seen him take food from," the old man explained. He looked up from under his graying eyebrows and pierced Farrell with a speculative look. "The only person outside of the family, that is."

Farrell looked a little surprised at that.

"Well, maybe he's just doing me a favor," he suggested, shrugging it off. "One stray to another, so to speak."

McKendrick laughed and moved a checker.

"Maybe," he said agreeably. "Then again, maybe not."

Farrell decided it might be wiser to sidestep the treacherous conversational waters that Loren seemed to be pursuing. In Farrell's experience, sometimes it was better to keep one's mouth shut. This had all of the earmarks of one of those times.

Kate listened patiently until the end of Jason's saga and ooh'd and aah'd at all the right places. Jason, immensely proud of his audience's reaction, rewarded her with a big hug, a wet kiss, and a heartfelt "I love you, Mommy."

"Okay, tiger. Time for a bath and bed," Kate declared.

"Can I say good night to Matt and Grandpa after?" he pleaded.

"Sure, sweetie," Kate soothed as she herded him gently in the direction of the bathroom.

"I don't know why I always hafta have a bath," he grumbled.

Kate raised her eyes heavenward and prayed for strength.

Farrell watched them disappear down the hall. It gave him a strange sensation. For a moment he'd almost thought it was *his* home, *his* family. . . . The warmth and banter, the caring and arguing . . . all his to share in. He blinked and looked back at the checkerboard.

When Jason scampered back across the room a little while later, the men were into their fourth game.

"Night," Jason crowed, giving his grandfather a big kiss and hug. Then, a little less confidently, he approached Farrell. "Night, Matt," he said.

Then he climbed onto Matt's lap and hugged him. As fast as he'd come he scrambled down and dashed off to his room.

"Now read me a story!" he cried to his mother as he rounded the bend.

Kate, who'd been standing in the hallway, was touched by the peculiar look in Matt's eyes.

"He's a nice kid," Farrell mumbled awkwardly when he realized that she'd been looking at him.

"And you're a nice man," she said with an easy smile.

Farrell grimaced and shook his head.

"Take off your rose-colored glasses!" he mumbled darkly, turning his attention back to the checkerboard in self-defense.

Kate took a deep breath and followed her son into his room. Farrell might be tough on the outside, she thought, but he was one tender man underneath, even if he *was* trying to deny it! He'd worn that darned poker face so long he'd come to believe it was him!

"Well you better watch out, Matt Farrell," she said under her breath, " 'cause your mask has slipped and I've seen what's underneath!"

Her lips curved into a secret smile.

And I like what I saw, she added mentally. I like what I saw.

The phone rang while Kate was reading Jason's bedtime story. It was Amos Mallory.

"Who's winning?" Kate inquired a short time later when she rejoined the men in the parlor.

"It's a draw," Loren said with a grimace. "I must be getting old!" He slowly got to his feet and stretched. "Maybe an extra hour's sleep'd help." He gave Farrell a friendly, challenging eye. "Try it again tomorrow?"

"Sure," he said amiably.

Kate stood awkwardly in the middle of the room as the elder McKendrick left. She wanted to run over to Farrell and throw her arms around him and kiss him. She could hardly do that! Especially in her father-in-law's presence. A shadow chased across her face. She wished it were different. She wished that very much.

Farrell watched her through half-closed eyes. He'd been

151

hanging around playing checkers with Loren twice as long as he really wanted to for one reason and one reason only—to be alone with Kate. And there she was standing halfway across the room from him looking like she didn't know what to say to him!

Maybe she was already beginning to regret the change in their relationship, he thought with a sinking heart. He managed a cynical smile. It wouldn't be the first time he'd been disappointed in life.

But he had to admit, this disappointment could leave scars deep enough to last a lifetime.

"Amos called," he told her as he played with the checkers.

Kate was startled out of her unhappy thoughts.

"So soon?" she asked.

"Yes. We got lucky. Walker went to a banking convention and word got around that he'd made a couple of big mistakes in the past year. A bad loan that will just about wipe out his reserves and an acquisition of a small savings and loan that's not turning out to be as lucrative as he hoped. In short, he's strapped for cash. If he can't come up with it by the time the auditors come through in six months, it'll be common knowledge."

Kate walked over to sit across from Farrell.

"It's hard to believe," she murmured, having a hard time taking it all in. "Everyone thinks he can do no financial wrong. . . . Why nearly all the town and half of the county do their banking with him! This could be devastating to the community."

"Federal insurance will soften the blow to the individual account holders for the most part. But Walker stands to be wiped out. He personally put up some of the collateral needed to secure the loan. If the collateral is called in he'll be lucky if he escapes with the shirt on his back and a couple of years in rent money."

"Good heavens!"

Farrell dropped the checkers back on the board and stood up, stuffing his hands into his pants pockets.

"You can see why he's interested in your land . . . especially if there's some gold on it."

Kate nodded faintly.

"Yes. I'm afraid I can," she admitted sadly.

She could remember the first time she'd met Sam Walker. It had been at a 4-H fair when she was seven. He'd let her ride in his carriage. She'd been so thrilled. He'd been very kind to her. She wondered if any vestige of that man she'd first met was still in Samuel Walker today. Somehow, she couldn't imagine the old Sam Walker getting himself into such a desperate situation. He had been too careful for something like that. But when had it begun, she wondered. When?

"A penny for your thoughts," Farrell said.

Kate shook her head.

"They're free," she said. "I was just wondering if Sam Walker bore any relationship to the man by that name I first met years ago. I guess time changes all of us in one way or another."

Farrell could see Kate's reflection in the window. It had been a peculiarly bittersweet experience being with her all day. He kept wanting to touch her, to kiss her. He'd forced himself to hold back for the most part.

The later it got, however, the harder it was for him to keep his mind off of it. He kept remembering the previous night . . . the taste of her lips, the feel of her skin, the incredible pleasure of making love to her . . . of being loved in return.

Kate sensed he was struggling with himself about something, but for the life of her she couldn't figure out exactly what. He had withdrawn from her in a subtle way. It shook her own confidence considerably. She didn't know what to expect if she moved toward him. She had the sinking feeling he might rebuff her. If he did that there wasn't much more to be said.

She wondered if he'd decided to avoid any further intimate entanglements with her.

She bit her lip and tried to think what to do.

Maybe it would be best to just clear the air, she thought, although she was not particularly thrilled at meeting this problem head on. She stood up and crossed her arms.

"Is something wrong, Matt?" she asked tentatively.

Everything is wrong, he wanted to say, but it sounded too ridiculous to utter, so he pushed the thought aside. She looked so vulnerable standing there with her arms crossed and her eyes wide open like a doe in the forest. . . . And suddenly he didn't give a damn about the awkward situation he'd gotten himself into. So he was falling for a widow tied firmly to her roots out in the middle of nowhere, he told himself. To hell with it, he thought. I'm just going to take it as it comes, one day at a time, and forget about what happens next! That will just have to take care of itself! He'd certainly had enough practice living like that over the years. He ought to be able to manage it well enough now, he told himself.

He walked up to her until they were only a foot apart and gave her long braid an affectionate tug. He rested his forearms on top of her shoulders and kissed her slowly and very thoroughly on the mouth.

"Not anymore," he murmured huskily as he lifted his lips a few mintues later. "Could I talk you into coming back to my place for a nightcap, Katherine Solace?" He pulled her into his arms and nuzzled her throat persuasively.

Kate moaned in spite of herself.

"On one condition," she managed to say.

"What's that?"

"That the nightcap doesn't turn out to be three-day-old coffee," she gasped as his tongue began tracing lazy, erotic circles on the sensitive interior of her ear. A thrill of delight coursed from the ear straight down through her middle. She clutched him convulsively and urgently sought his mouth with hers.

Farrell laughed softly and willingly succumbed to the pleasure of kissing her back.

"That wasn't exactly the kind of nightcap I had in mind," he admitted, his breath warming her lips when he broke the kiss. "Let's go before I tear your clothes off you and demonstrate what I had in mind right in the middle of the parlor," he suggested as he raked her from head to toe with burning eyes.

He grabbed their coats and clasped Kate's hand in his.

They didn't let go of each other again for quite a long, satisfying time.

It was breakfast as usual the following morning. The aroma of bacon and fresh coffee, homemade biscuits and country-fried potatoes laced the air with savory promise. Jason was stuffing his mouth for the last time when Farrell finally joined them.

Kate thought he looked wonderful.

"Good morning," she said happily as she set a plate before him.

"Good morning," he replied, the warm glance he returned to her saying far more than his words. "Sleep well?" he asked blandly as he reached for the homemade jam.

Kate blushed and made a face at him over Jason's innocent head. She'd exhausted herself in his arms and he most certainly knew it! She could just barely remember stripping off her clothes once she'd gotten back to her own bedroom. She must have fallen asleep as she'd fallen into her bed!

"Where's Loren?" Farrell asked. It was unusual for him not to be at the table.

"His hip was acting up again," she explained. "He's soaking in a hot tub. It's never really mended right since he broke it a few years ago. Old bones aren't quite as resilient as young ones."

Farrell nodded sympathetically and dug into the tasty, freshly cooked food. The restaurant meals he'd downed over the years made him especially appreciate eating at Kate's table. There was something especially relaxing and enjoyable about eating in the tight-knit atmosphere of this family home. The warmth didn't just come from the food. It came from the heart.

Jason wiped a napkin over his little hands at the speed of light and mumbled something about going to see if Doc would play catch with him for a while.

"I can't understand you when you talk with your mouth full!" his mother called after him as he ran through the parlor on his way outside.

Kate shook her head helplessly and cleared away Jason's messy plates.

"Oh, well," she sighed. "Maybe they can get him to listen in kindergarten next year."

Farrell grinned and started buttering another mouth-watering buttermilk biscuit.

"I seem to recall hearing my mother say the same thing when I was a kid," he offered in Jason's defense. "When it matters to him he can speak plainly enough."

Kate laughed and joined him for a cup of coffee.

"Too plainly," she agreed, ruefully recalling a few choice words he'd tried out on his Sunday-school friends of late.

Kate watched Farrell eat, enjoying the chance to sit with him. There was a quiet intimacy about sitting together at the

155

breakfast table. Kate felt it and so did Farrell. Even the silences were warm and trusting, like links in a chain, forging them a little closer together.

Farrell cleared his own dishes away and sat down in the chair next to Kate to finish his coffee. He casually draped an arm along the back of her chair, more than pleased that he had her to himself for a little bit.

"I missed you after you left last night," he said quietly, tracing a slow path on the back of her neck with the tips of his fingers. He leaned forward and pulled her chin gently toward him. "I've been wanting to do this ever since I walked in the dining room," he murmured huskily.

He gave her a warm, searching kiss, awakening in her again all the longing she always felt when he touched her. She relaxed into him and he took full advantage of her surrender.

They were interrupted by a man's voice calling from the front porch as he stuck his head inside.

"Kate? McKendrick? It's Vern Peterson. Y'all decent?"

Farrell pulled away and Kate took a deep breath to get back on an even keel.

"Next time, don't wait so long," Kate teased Farrell, laying a kiss on her fingertips and placing them lightly against his lips. She stood up and put the palms of her hands on her face in a small effort to cool her burning cheeks. "Come in, Vern," she called out as she walked into the parlor.

Farrell got up and followed her, wondering what kind of reception to expect this time from Still Waters's resident chief of law and order.

The reception he got was reluctant civility.

Vern didn't bother to try to hide the fact that underneath the official neutrality ran a vein of resentment and uncertainty about Farrell. Farrell was a man's man as well as a woman's man. He had a tough, silent-type way about him that western men thought of as raw, masculine strength. At the same time he had a virility and understated appeal that women found utterly fascinating. Vern was smart enough to have noticed both aspects.

He gave Farrell an abrupt nod.

"Mornin', Farrell. I heard you were back in town," he said

156

coolly. Vern turned his attention to Kate. "Is he workin' for you again, Kate?"

Kate was caught by surprise. It wasn't the question as much as the tone of voice that startled her. There was a stiffness in Vern Peterson's voice that usually wasn't there. If she hadn't known better, she'd have said Vern was jealous that Farrell was staying with her . . . that he was hoping the gambler was working for her, not being a friend to her instead.

But that was silly, she told herself. Vern and she had never been involved romantically. And she'd made it clear she didn't want to be. He'd always seemed quite able to live with that. There'd never been any hint that he was nursing some undying love for her. True, he'd expressed an interest in having her as a wife, but that was because he wanted a family and she met his minimum requirements. Men! she thought in frustration. They don't necessarily want the bone that badly themselves . . . but they don't want anyone else sniffing after it either!

"No, Vern. This time he's visiting and doing a little hunting," she said easily, glancing impishly in Farrell's direction as she mentioned hunting.

Peterson nodded and gave Farrell a strange, speculative look. "Hm. Well, I rode up to the ridge yesterday and had a look around," the lawman said, running his fingers over the brim of his Stetson. "I found one set of horse prints and some empty cartridges. Whoever it was rode up into the mountains and into the ravines. I lost the trail on one of the rocky stretches where the river dries up at this time of year."

Kate nodded. At least Vern had found something, she thought hopefully. It wouldn't just be her word and Farrell's.

"It *could* have been somebody shootin' at *you*," he admitted, not too happily. "On the other hand, maybe whoever it was didn't see you and was shootin' at something else."

"Like what?" Farrell asked sarcastically. "We were easy to see at that range. The afternoon light was on us and we both had on dark coats."

"You aren't the only person who likes to hunt around here," Peterson argued sourly. "Lots of people do."

"How many like to hunt people, Sheriff?" Farrell asked with marked interest.

Vern glared at him and pulled his Stetson down on his head.

"By the way," the lawman added, addressing Kate, "when I was tracking him, I ran across some other prints that you might like to know about. Mountain lion. A good-sized one. You better watch out along the northeast edge of your property. That cat was comin' down pretty close. Your cattle are going to look mighty tasty to it."

"Thanks, Vern," Kate said gratefully.

She walked him to the porch and waved good-bye as he rode back down the hill toward town. A worried expression had come into her eyes. She couldn't afford to lose any cattle. That herd was all she had left. They had to calve and be ready to sell in the spring or she wouldn't have a chance to try her ace in the hole. The game would be all over before that particular card could be played!

"I'm going out again," she said, whistling for Doc and grabbing her heavy leather jacket. "If Vern's right about that cat, I'd better move the cattle closer in. It'll be easier to keep an eye on them down here until someone can spot the cat and eliminate it permanently from the neighborhood!" she sighed.

"I'll help," Farrell said, grabbing his own coat and following her to the barn.

They loaded their rifles this time.

It took all day but they brought the small herd back in. Kate had bought herself a little more of that most precious commodity—time. But she was beginning to have a sinking feeling in the pit of her stomach. She had the nagging feeling that her time was running out.

By the time they got back and took care of the horses it was well after dark. Loren and Jason had eaten and gone to bed, leaving some food for Kate and Farrell to warm up.

"Too tired to come back to my place for a last cup of coffee?" he asked quietly as they put away the last of the dishes and hung up the dish towels.

Kate looked at him in surprise. He'd sounded a little cooler than he had last night. Was he trying to avoid having her go with him? Letting her down politely? Like a true gentleman? she wondered in dismay.

Then she saw the expression in his eyes. He wanted her, all right, she realized in relief.

"No." She walked up to him, giving him a saucy look and

158

placing her hands on her hips. "I'm used to the fresh air and plenty of exercise, gambling man!" She walked closer and looped her arms around his waist. "We can really just have coffee, you know," she said gently, giving him a tender kiss on the cheek.

He pulled her close. Kate couldn't see the grin spreading across his face.

"That might be a good idea," he said, sounding very convincing. "I'm bushed. Why don't you come and help me rest my weary, city bones."

Kate was a little startled to see what he had in mind a short while later. It was when he started running the bath water that she began to get the first inkling.

"Ladies first," he suggested with a straight face. "I'll make some coffee."

Kate had to admit she'd feel a lot better after a nice hot bath. They'd worked hard rounding up cattle. Even in cold weather you began to smell like horse and leather. She wrinkled her nose and dropped her clothes by the large claw-foot bathtub that had been installed fifty years earlier along with the indoor plumbing.

When she was drying off a short while later, she was amused to note a masculine forearm being cautiously extended inside the partly opened door. A clean man's shirt was being offered.

"Thought you might like a change," Farrell explained.

He took his turn next.

She'd assumed he was finished, having heard the water drain out, when all of a sudden the taps were turned back on.

"Okay, ranch lady," he called out. "Come here and help soothe my bruised body."

Kate grinned and joined him, coffee in hand.

They drank the coffee while Kate rubbed his back and he soaked in the tub of deliciously warm water.

"You know," she said enviously, "you're a tricky man, Farrell." She was working on the long muscles running down his back on either side of his backbone. They were hard and tense but seemed to be loosening as her fingers pressed and stretched them.

"Tricky?" he growled in mock outrage. "I'm as straightforward as the day is long!" He was also immensely enjoying the feel of her hands as they played over the muscles of his back and shoulders. A man could really get spoiled into expecting this all the time, he thought, as pleasure and relaxation flowed through him in rhythm with her ministrations.

"Pretending to be a broken-down city boy just so I'd rub your back!" She cupped her hand in the clear, warm water and dribbled it over his unsuspecting face.

He turned so fast, so fluidly, she never had a chance. The next thing she knew he'd pulled her down into the tub on top of him and was laughing softly at her startled expression.

"Sorry. But I think I can find a way to make amends," he murmured persuasively.

Kate stared in fascination into his eyes. His body was warm and hard against hers. His hands had begun kneading the tender flesh of her back, working down from the shoulders. Kate groaned and closed her eyes in pleasure.

"Mmmm," she mumbled, relaxing against him. "I need lots of amends, Farrell," she sighed.

The soft laugh rumbling under her was overwhelmingly masculine to Kate's foggy senses. Like a big cat that had the mouse it wanted in its paws and was happily about to eat it.

His fingers worked over the muscles of her buttocks and thighs, drifting confidently into the sensitive inner surfaces. As he found tenderer flesh to explore she automatically clenched her fingers into his shoulders and searched for his mouth. As their lips fused, heating up everything considerably, his fingers were replaced by an even more welcome invasion.

"Mmmm," she moaned incoherently as they undulated into each other in slow, sweet tides of rising pleasure. "Mmmm."

His hands dug into her sides as the tides became waves. Thought blurred and there was only sensation. There was only joining together to give each other the supreme pleasure, the bond of joy. They cried out at the same moment, bodies convulsing in unison, arms bound tightly around each other, hearts full of the same emotion. And the last tidal wave crashed hard against them, throwing them into the peace that follows the storm.

"I think I'm going to need another shirt," Kate whispered a little later.

Farrell laughed and lifted her in his arms as he got out of the tub.

160

"I think that can be arranged," he chuckled, giving her swollen lips another deep, lingering kiss.

They dried off and half dressed, Kate in another one of Farrell's shirts, he in form-fitting underwear. They stretched out on the couch to have a last cup of coffee before calling it a night.

He caressed her hair, laying his head back against the arm of the couch and admiring again some of the antiques decorating the old cabin.

"Are those old branding irons?" he asked lazily, nodding toward the crossed iron poles mounted along one wall.

"Yes," Kate replied, following his line of vision. "They're an S and a W . . . short for Still Waters," she explained with a fond smile. "Still Waters was originally the name of this ranch. The town came along many years later and only kind of stole it. I guess by then it didn't matter much anymore to the family. This place has always been called the McKendrick ranch, anyway."

"Still Waters . . . that's an odd name for a brand . . . or for a ranch, isn't it?" he asked curiously. In all the years he'd been traveling around the West, Farrell couldn't recall ever having come across a spread by that name. A few towns, maybe, but no homes.

Kate leaned back, enjoying the feel of being cradled against him. Her head had a snug berth in the curve of his shoulder. His arm locked her gently against his side. Their left hands were laced together. All in all, she felt half woven to the man and she loved every moment of it.

"The story goes," she began, her eyes going slightly out of focus as she visualized what she was speaking of, "that John McKendrick wanted to find a peaceful place to live and raise a family. He'd met Katherine in the gold frenzy of 1850 and had killed a man who'd tried to rape her. She'd lost her only living relative in the trek across the Sierras trying to get to the gold-mining camps. Her father had dragged her along and then fallen off a mountain before he'd ever even seen a nugget!" Kate shook her head at the irony of it.

"Being a woman alone around the mining camps must have been pretty rough," Farrell said sympathetically.

"Very rough," Kate agreed. "But she had a skill that gave her some extra value and probably helped keep some of the nastier characters at bay. Her father had been a miner in the East, and she'd learned how to separate gold from gravel. In the early days people just dug into the rivers with their pans and scooped the gold out. Later they began to realize how much they were losing. Katherine could work downstream from any number of miners and still make a good living for herself. That gained her the respect of enough men in the camp she was in for her to be protected by the camp's laws."

"Until someone noticed that there are things in this world besides gold?" Farrell asked with a very masculine grin.

"Yes. Fortunately, she'd met and fallen in love with John McKendrick by then and he saved her from all that."

Farrell put his coffee cup down on the floor and shifted Kate slightly, bringing them into a more comfortable position. He gave her a soft kiss on the throat and smiled at her.

"If the picture is anything like her, she was a beautiful woman . . . just like her namesake."

Kate gave him a radiant smile and ran a playful hand across the hard muscles of his abdomen.

"Why thank you, sir," she said coquettishly.

"Tell me, how did you come to be named after her, anyway?" he asked in consternation. "That's been driving me nuts!"

Kate grinned.

"She's an ancestor of mine," she replied simply.

Farrell hesitated. He hadn't expected that to be the reason, but he wasn't slow to see the obvious implication.

"You're related to the McKendricks by blood?" he asked slowly.

There was something about delving into her family that left him ill at ease. He knew what it was too. Her late husband. He didn't know how much he cared to learn about that man. He was inclined to think that the less he knew, the better he'd like it.

"Yes. Very distant cousins. John and Katherine had five children. The eldest boy stayed and took over this ranch. The next eldest child, a girl, married and carved out the ranch next to it . . . the one that belonged to my folks. . . . I grew up there, but I practically spent as much time here at the McKendricks' as I did at my own house," she reminisced with a smile.

She'd grown up with Seth. It seemed like an eternity ago to

her now. Almost like another lifetime. They'd done chores together, gone to school together, learned about growing up together. He'd been her first and only lover, until Farrell.

"How did your husband die, Kate?" Farrell asked.

Kate was startled at the question, coming as it had out of the blue. She'd expected that sooner or later Farrell might ask. She was glad they'd finally gotten around to it. It was like a bridge they had to cross before they could go on with their journey, she thought.

"Seth . . . Seth never really felt the same way as I did about the ranches," she explained slowly, trying to find the right words to make him understand. "He loved the freedom out here, the peace, the independence . . . but he had an itch to see a little more of the world. He'd gone into San Francisco to look into jobs down at the docks." She shook her head sadly. "He always had this dream that he'd be a seaman for a year, see the world, and then come home and ranch for the rest of his life. I don't think he'd ever really have gone. . . . By then Jason had just been born, and Seth knew he was needed here, but he always had that dream."

Farrell was surprised to hear the sympathy and understanding in Kate's voice.

"Most women would have found that kind of dream pretty abominable, I would think," he pointed out. "It would have meant leaving you to fend for yourself for quite a while."

Kate shrugged philosophically.

"I didn't feel that way. We'd known each other forever. I wanted him to get it out of his system, do it while he could. His father was in better health then, so there would have been two of us here . . . my folks and my sister and her husband were still next to us . . . Seth thought we'd all be okay without him."

Farrell shook his head in amazement.

"It never happened," she said softly. "He was having a beer in a waterfront bar with a stranger when a knife fight broke out. Seth pushed the stranger out of harm's way and was knifed in his stead. He died on the operating table a little while later." She sighed and shut her eyes. "It was such a waste! He had everything to live for. . . ." It always made her angry to think of it.

163

Farrell's arms tightened protectively around her.

"I'm sorry, Kate," he murmured against her cheek.

She nodded and held on to him, drawing comfort from him. And then something seemed to melt inside of her, and she felt the tears slide gently down her cheeks. Farrell didn't say any more. He just held her until the tears were spent.

"You know," she whispered, "I feel like I finally said good-bye to him."

Farrell leaned his jaw against hers and pressed her head close. Sometimes there simply weren't words to be said.

CHAPTER TEN

Kate actually did take Farrell hunting the next day. They tried their luck at tracking the big cat stalking the fringes of the ranch. The mountain lion was an elusive quarry, however. Even Doc couldn't help them pin her down.

Just before they turned back toward home, however, a distant scream split the air. It curdled the blood and sent shivers down the back. There was an unearthly quality to it. The sound it most resembled was that of a woman's scream.

Farrell twisted in his saddle and raised the binoculars to his eyes.

"See her?" Kate asked, shielding her own eyes and squinting into the distance.

"No." He stuffed the binoculars back into their case and gathered the reins with one hand. "I have the feeling that cat's been sitting up there somewhere watching us look for her all day. She was just having the last laugh!" he said wryly.

Kate smiled cheerlessly and nodded her head.

"It sure sounded that way, didn't it?" she agreed as they rode back. "That's fine by me. She can laugh and yowl all she likes . . . just so long as she stays away from my cattle!"

For the time being, she did. The cattle foraged peacefully, unaware that they were being considered for a hungry predator's menu. Kate breathed another sigh of relief at the end of the day. One more day safely passed.

She was just about to leave the barn late one evening when Farrell unexpectedly joined her.

She smiled in welcome, but the happy expression slowly faded as she noted his serious demeanor. All day he'd been a little more preoccupied than usual, she'd thought. She'd put it down to pregame nerves. His poker showdown with T.J. was tomorrow.

Now, as she watched him absently slap a leather strap against his open palm, she wasn't so sure. Maybe there was something else. . . .

"Ready for tomorrow?" she asked, latching the mare's stall door and leaning back against it.

Farrell shrugged noncommittally.

"I suppose you could say that," he replied vaguely. "You never really know what luck's going to hand you in a poker hand," he pointed out. "So it isn't something you can really train for."

"I see what you mean."

"You have to have the right attitude, though," he continued slowly. "That is one thing you can try to work on. Some people have better luck at it than others."

She eyed him thoughtfully.

"I don't know much about playing poker for a living," she said slowly, "but I would think a pro who wins big over the years has an excellent attitude, as you put it. I would have called it self-discipline, maybe. Is that the same thing?"

Farrell ran a hand over the back of his neck. He'd been working on this speech for days. Today in particular he'd forced himself actually to think of the words to use with Kate. But now he was here and he couldn't say them. They stuck in his throat, not wanting to be said. But damn it all, he had to say them. They had just about run out of time, and he didn't want to leave Kate without some sort of farewell.

He didn't really want to leave her at all, he realized, with a twist of pain in his heart. He'd known that unconsciously for a long time now. But he couldn't see any future for them. Kate's life was here in the foothills and mountains, raising her son, living off the land. His life was in the bright lights of big-city gambling establishments. How in the hell could those two ever mesh?

He'd asked himself that a dozen times. Each time a stubborn, pragmatic voice had whispered that there was no way. He was an outsider. He'd never fit in here. And Kate would never fit in where he did. He didn't even want to ask her to try. It wasn't a great place to be, as far as he was concerned. He'd gotten used to it over the years, though. He hoped he'd be able to go back to it without remembering what he couldn't have. Before he'd met Kate he'd been happy enough, he supposed. Now he knew what he'd be missing. Knowing was a terrible thing, in this case.

"Discipline?" he echoed. Yeah, Farrell, he told himself scornfully. Let's see some discipline! "That's a good word for it, I guess," he agreed. "You have to know for yourself that it doesn't matter what's lying on the table when the betting starts. If you can't lose a bet, you shouldn't be in the game. The night before a high-stakes game you have to know where you stand on that particular issue. If you don't give a damn about the cash, the material possessions or security it represents . . . you're okay."

Kate stared at him, trying to read what was behind this. He was still not telling her. She was sure of that. It was a chilling realization. In her experience, when people tried to avoid getting to the point it usually meant there was bad news of some sort. She licked her lips and cocked her head to one side.

"That sounds pretty reckless," she said uncertainly.

"No. If you're reckless, you throw away your capital, and you don't make it to the high-stakes arenas of poker playing," he said. He held her gaze steadily, trying to soften the blow. "Poker is something I'm good at. I've been a winner more often than a loser when it counted because I knew the odds and I wasn't afraid to play them to the hilt. If your feelings obscure your objectivity . . . if you can't calculate the odds accurately . . . you're in big trouble. And if you know the odds are against you and you still bet everything you have on a hand, you're out of business. You'll lose."

Kate heard the low, even voice and every word uttered, but she had the feeling he wasn't just talking about poker anymore. He was staring at her intently. For a second she thought she'd seen pain flicker in those hazel depths. Then the mask had slipped over and she couldn't be sure.

"What are we talking about, Matt?" she asked, fearing to hear the answer now.

He watched her lift her chin as she asked. Like a fighter getting ready to take a punch on the jaw . . . or daring an opponent to land one there. He grimaced and pressed his lips together in a hard, unhappy line before forcing himself to make it clear.

Once it was said there would be no going back. He knew that.

He walked toward her, crossing the room in slow, measured strides, like a man going to his own execution. When he reached her he cupped her head tenderly in his hands and kissed her softly on the mouth.

"After the game's over, I'm leaving, Kate," he said.

His voice was low and even and aching with pain. The words hurt too much for Kate to hear the pain, however.

She pulled a little away and blinked. She'd never really thought about the future with him. She'd taken it one day at a time. But foolishly, deep in her heart, she'd felt it would go on forever. She hadn't known how they'd manage to do it, but she'd trusted that they'd have found a way. He was such a part of her heart now, she couldn't imagine his really leaving for good.

"Why the rush?" was all she could think to say, stunned as she was by his blunt announcement.

"Because my whole life is beyond this ranch," he forced himself to say. "And your whole life is on it."

Kate couldn't believe her ears.

"That's it?" she asked in pained disbelief. "That's it?" She pulled back, freeing herself from his loose grasp.

"Damn it, Kate! What would I do here? What would you do in Reno?" he bellowed, his own misery boiling up in anger and spilling over. "If we'd met fifteen years ago, maybe things would be different! I could have tried to be a part of a community, be a normal citizen just paying his taxes and praying for rain and good beef prices like everyone else around here! But that's not the way it was. I make my living off people like you. My friends are as close to riffraff as you can get and still be out of jail!"

She grabbed the collar of his coat and stood on tiptoe to look him in the eye as best she could.

"I don't care about any of that!" she cried angrily. "You can go on playing poker until the cows come home!" she swore. "Travel all over the world to every big poker game known to man for all I care!" Her eyes flashed like hot emeralds from the depth of her frustration with him. "Live in Reno five nights a week and fleece every farmer stupid enough to think he can best a savvy pro at his own game! I don't give a *damn* about them! Just don't use that as an excuse to forget about *us*, Matt Farrell!"

He wanted so badly to let her talk him into it, he could almost taste it. But she was beautiful, and gutsy, and would take on anything without a thought to herself.

"I couldn't see you go through that," he said softly, tracing the curve of her cheek with his hand. "Eventually you'd become disillusioned, angry—"

"It's my life, Matt! If I'm willing to chance it, why won't you?" she cried out.

He knew exactly why, but he was not about to give her that last piece of ammunition to use against him. He wasn't sure how long he could stand up against her if she knew how close he was to giving in against his better judgment.

"It's not worth it, honey," he said softly, gently removing her hands from his jacket front.

She flinched as if he'd struck her.

He'd used every ounce of discipline he had to say those words, and he'd produced an Oscar-winning performance. There was firmness in his voice, a touch of pity in his eyes, and an underlying steely quality of determination that told her there was nothing more to say.

Kate's pride came somewhat to her rescue. She'd never been the type to dissolve in the face of a disappointment. Even so, the hurt was there to see in her face.

"I . . . see," she managed to say. She stood as if frozen. "I guess I got a little carried away . . ." she said jerkily, swallowing hard and trying to think of what to say under the circumstances. She'd been so sure he really cared. . . .

She slipped away from him and headed for the door, hesitating just before leaving.

"I'm sorry it isn't worth it to you," she said in a choked voice, her back still to him. "Because it would have been worth it to me. But then, I fell in love with you." She raised her face upward as if searching for a fate to blame. "How unbelievably stupid of me!"

He heard the sob at the end of her angry last exclamation, and it tore into him like a knife.

Kate threw open the barn door and started walking up the hill. Within a few steps, her head bowed, she began to run.

"Kate!" he cried, running after her.

She was in the house before he could reach her. He tried the doorknob, but found it already locked. He pounded on the door and called after her.

"Kate!"

He thought he heard a sound, like muffled sobs. He leaned his forehead against the door in defeat. He was sure he'd done the right thing. Kate was a beautiful, wonderful woman. She'd forget him and find someone else.

He closed his eyes in pain and hit the door with his fist.

He didn't want her to find someone else, damn it! And he wanted to go even less than he had before!

Farrell forced himself to straighten up and head back toward his own quarters. Every step of the way, her sobs tormented him. And the memory of everything she'd said lacerated his thoughts. Especially the last thing she'd said . . . that she loved him.

He kept telling himself he'd done the right thing. He'd done her the biggest favor he could.

Nothing could take the pain away from him, though. The soul-wrenching ache in his chest was almost unbearable.

"Mommy!" cried an exuberant small voice. "Can I go too?"

Kate checked to see that the saddle rested comfortably on the mare and then swung up into it. She bent down and gave the eager little boy an affectionate tousling on the head with one hand.

"Maybe next time, honey," she promised with a smile.

She was going out to see just how close that cat had come last night, and she didn't want Jason hanging on behind her until she knew the answer.

"Aw, Mom!" he wailed protestingly, giving her a very annoyed look.

"After that cat goes back where she belongs, Jason," Kate told him, holding her hand over her heart to swear she meant it. "Why don't you take Doc and try and build a snowman?"

Jason knew she was trying to change the subject and pouted

rebelliously. But he did love to build snowmen . . . and snow castles and snow everythings!

"Okay!" He hopped over to the bottom of the porch steps and tried to whistle for the dog. The blowing sound didn't produce any noticeable sound and he gave up in disgust and called Doc's name.

Farrell came out of the old homestead in time to see Kate turn Calamity's head toward the range.

"You're starting early," he said, gazing steadily at her.

Her slim figure stayed erect and proud. She looked down at him as he walked toward her.

"Good morning," she said, staring back at him enigmatically.

He had to hand it to her. She had a lot of discipline herself. He could see she was tired and not too happy. She wasn't going to give in to him, though. She was going to go out and try and get on with her life, no matter how much she was hurting.

"Matt's going to be going pretty soon, Jason," she said somberly. She knew how much Jason liked Farrell and wished she could have at least spared Jason the pain of losing a friend. "Maybe you should spend a little time saying good-bye today."

Jason's little face fell in disappointment.

"Aw, gee . . ."

She looked back at Matt and took a deep breath.

"Good luck," she said calmly. "If I don't see you when you get back, I guess this is good-bye as well."

Farrell reached up as if to hold the mare's bridle. Kate saw the motion and dug her heels into the mare's sides. She bolted away before he could do anything about it.

"Kate!" he shouted.

She didn't even look back.

Farrell ground his teeth together and frowned in unhappy frustration at her disappearing figure. He reminded himself that he'd made his own bed. Now he had to lie in the cold, lonely thing!

Jason scampered over to Farrell and grabbed his hand, knowing how grown-ups tended to find ingenious excuses to avoid some serious playing!

"Can you teach me some new card tricks? Please?" he begged.

Farrell slowly turned his attention back to the small boy next to him. He'd grown very fond of the curly-haired little rascal. It was easy to do with a child as lively and fun-loving as Kate's little boy.

"Sure, Jason." He smiled.

Doc trotted along after them as they went back to the old homestead. When the card tricks began the dog curled comfortably at the gambler's feet as if it were the most natural place in the world for him to be.

The Still Waters card parlor was full to overflowing by late morning. Everyone in town had managed to come up with an excuse for stopping by. No one really believed the reasons, of course. Everyone knew the truth.

T.J. and Farrell were having a rematch. No one wanted to miss that.

In spite of the clean clothes and indoor setting, the atmosphere was reminiscent of a dogfight. People just couldn't help wanting to see whose blood would be spilled, who would vanquish whom. There were even side bets being surreptitiously placed on the outcome in low-voiced conversations scattered around the hall.

T.J. was slapping longtime buddies on the back and pinching former high school girlfriends here and there. But when Farrell walked in a vicious light kindled in T.J.'s eyes. He'd have been happier to have agreed to a fistfight than another poker game. There was something about Farrell that stuck in his gut like a sharp, painful burr. He wanted to cut it out once and for all and turn his attention to conquering the things he so dearly coveted.

T.J. gave Farrell a snakelike smile.

"Glad to see you could make it, Farrell," he said, just barely slurring the words enough to give them an insulting tone. "Surprised you wanted to try this again."

Farrell shrugged and eyed his opponent with absolute neutrality.

"I don't see why," Farrell said evenly. "Last time I won in a big way."

Farrell looked around the room as if interested in the decor. It hadn't changed from the last time. Deer horns were mounted along one wall. An old placer miner's pan was hung not too far away from it. Country and western music was crooning softly in the background, piped in from the diner next door. The walls were rustic, along with the chairs and lamps.

Not only hadn't it changed from the last time, Farrell thought dryly, it looked like it probably hadn't changed in twenty or thirty years.

Farrell drew a long cigarillo from the inside of his pocket and ambled over to the playing table. He struck a long match against the sole of his shoe and lit the tobacco, cupping the flame with his match hand.

"I'm ready whenever you are," he said easily, drawing and exhaling a thin stream of smoke.

T.J. nodded and directed the crowd to step back, clear of the center of action.

Farrell knew T.J.'s type. He wasn't surprised by the boisterousness or the hale-fellow-well-met attitude. T.J. was the type to keep up a string of comments during a game . . . throwing in occasional off-color jokes and sexual innuendos to try to divert his opponent's concentration.

Farrell would have laughed if he hadn't been so deeply angry at the man. He wanted T.J.'s hide! Nothing less would satisfy his thirst for revenge. Until that need was met there would be no laughter.

"California Lowball with the bug," T.J. said, announcing the game they'd agreed to. "Cut to see who deals?"

Farrell nodded.

T.J. opened a new deck and cut, showing the bottom card faceup. It was a ten of spades.

Farrell took his cut and turned up a card. The queen of hearts.

T.J. leaned back and began reciting a tale he claimed to find amusing. Farrell took it the way it was meant—patter to try to divert Farrell's attention.

You'll have to try something better than that, Farrell thought as he shuffled the deck and offered the cards for his opponent to cut.

They each anted and Farrell dealt them five cards apiece.

T.J. looked at his cards and reached for the pile of cash he'd deposited beside him on the table.

"I'll open with a hundred dollars," he said with a bearish grin, slapping the single bill down on the pot in the middle.

173

Farrell lifted the front edge of his five cards. Without expression he reached for his own cash.

"I'll see your hundred, and raise you a hundred."

Amos Mallory slipped into the back of the crowd just in time to hear Farrell's first bet. He wasn't about to let his son face this particular opponent alone. He'd been in gambling long enough to know crooks when he ran across them. This time Farrell would have his own troops around if he needed them, Mallory thought grimly.

This time it would be a game of skill and strategy, fair and square. If it wasn't, someone would answer to the two big bruisers who'd quietly followed Amos Mallory into the card parlor!

Kate rode to the far northeast corner of her ranch. The cold wind poured down the mountainside, cascading across the foothills and valleys like an arctic river. She wrapped her scarf more snugly around her neck and pulled up her gloves a little to protect her wrists more.

She'd seen evidence that a mountain lion had prowled the area. Scat and paw prints and the bloody remains of a small animal were telltale proof. It was a good thing they'd moved the cattle when they did, she thought. Otherwise, it would be dead cattle carcasses she'd be finding instead. Eventually the cattle might have stampeded through a fence in their efforts to escape the hungry carnivore. And there she'd be, the proud owner of cattle running in every direction all over the northeast part of the state!

She laughed in good humor. At least there was one problem she didn't have yet, she thought gratefully.

She shielded her eyes and tried to make out the freshness of the trail she'd found. It looked like it was a half day old or so, she guessed. She checked the rifle for the fourth time and slid it back into place.

"Come on, Calam," she said, clucking softly to the mare and urging her forward. "The cat's full now. She's not gonna be hungry for us!"

The mare's ears flicked forward attentively and she pranced a little in excitement.

Kate laughed softly.

"Just don't waste all your energy dancing for joy about that! We still might need to move fast if we find her!"

The mare trotted north as Kate followed the trail left by the cat. She couldn't help remembering the last time she'd gone hunting. Farrell had come with her.

She forced herself to see the prints and keep a sharp eye out for danger up ahead. But Matt's face kept intruding, haunting her. Kate bit her lip until tears came to her eyes. She couldn't do anything about him, she told herself bleakly. He was doing what he wanted right this very minute. And he'd made it abundantly clear that he wanted to do it without her.

"You're a fool, Matt Farrell!" she cried out when she couldn't stand it any longer. "And I guess I must be too, to love you like I do!"

She wiped the tears away with the woolen scarf. She knew she didn't need frostbite on top of everything else! Then she gritted her teeth and forced herself to concentrate on the cat. She was looking so hard at the ground to accomplish that, she didn't notice a small bloody carcass stretched in the snow not too far away. Nor the horse prints within throwing distance from it.

Farrell leaned back and inhaled slowly. He savored the aroma of the cigarillo and slowly, reluctantly exhaled it.

T.J. was leaning on his elbows, waiting for Farrell to do something. He was still the expansive big-mouth as far as his friends and neighbors could see. But to Farrell's trained eye, he'd begun to sweat. The tiny habit T.J. had of twisting his lower jaw slightly to one side was a dead giveaway. He was as nervous as hell, Farrell thought in satisfaction. Farrell intended to draw that out and use it.

"Well?" T.J. prompted, for the first time a hint of annoyance in his voice. "What're you gonna do, Farrell? Fish or cut bait?" The slightly insulting, swaggering tone was back full force.

"Well, T.J.," Farrell said smoothly, restraining the urge to let a gleam of triumph show in his eyes. "I think maybe I'll see that five hundred." He shoved the money forward. He hesitated and added, almost apologetically, "And I'll raise you five hundred more."

T.J. couldn't believe it. He bluffed a lot at cards. Most people backed down. Somehow, Farrell backed off only when T.J.'s hands were winners. Now, when he'd gone out on a limb with two pair, Farrell was going to stick it to him!

T.J. glanced at the faces of the townspeople around him. They thought of him as a big-time poker player. He'd been fleecing them one way or another for years. He couldn't let Farrell beat him. Once had been infuriating. Twice would be more humiliation than T.J. cared to take in a lifetime. No, somehow, he'd have to outmaneuver the gambler.

T.J. shoved his money in and called.

Farrell spread his cards. Nine high. He won.

T.J. slapped his cards down and watched Farrell rake in the winnings. If lady luck wasn't on his side today, he'd have to make his own, T.J. decided coldly.

Sam Walker sat in a big wooden chair in a nearby corner and watched as T.J. shuffled and dealt. He saw the hard shadow of a smile on his son's face and wondered what he had up his sleeve.

Farrell watched T.J. deal and realized something was a little different in the way T.J. was handling the cards. He took a closer look and recognized what it was. T.J. had switched the way he was holding the pack. Now he was using the card mechanic's grip.

So you're going to cheat, huh? Farrell mused to himself as he looked at his cards.

They anted and Farrell wondered in amusement what sloppy form of card manipulation T.J. was going to try. If he was trying to cheat, he must be getting worried, Farrell thought with satisfaction.

T.J., I'm going to let you have enough rope to hang yourself, Farrell said to himself. I'll be happy to give you the final push in a couple more hands.

T.J.'s eyes gleamed as he began placing his bets. His was not a poker face.

Mallory had been watching the play of each hand intently. He couldn't figure out why Farrell had allowed T.J. to win the last two. It had restored some of T.J.'s losses, which Mallory hated to see. He'd immediately seen T.J.'s change of grip. He'd also seen T.J. dealing seconds instead of straight off the top . . . taking a peek a couple of times as well when he was pretending to check his cards. Amos was sure that Matt had noticed it too. Farrell's eyes were too sharp to miss it. What he couldn't figure out was why Farrell was letting T.J. cheat him!

As T.J. happily raked in his winnings Farrell leaned forward and put out the stub of his cigarillo.

"That's really some string of luck you're having," Farrell said with feigned admiration. "And you know, I think I know what I need to get back in the game."

T.J. looked at him suspiciously.

"What's that?" he asked unsympathetically.

"Well," Farrell said evenly, "sometimes I do better when the stakes are a little higher."

T.J. could not believe his ears.

"You want to raise the stakes?" he asked in disbelief.

Farrell nodded and grinned coldly.

"Yeah." He hesitated for a moment, as if issuing a subtle challenge. "Say five thousand to ante, five more to bet, ten to raise and call. If that's not too steep for you, of course."

T.J.'s face lit up like a Christmas tree and his beady little eyes were fairly alight with glee.

"Sure," he drawled in his best ole-boy baritone. "That's okay with me!"

T.J. reached for the cards but was stopped as Farrell's hand clamped down on his.

"Oh, one other thing," the gambler said, looking straight at T.J. "I think we could use a new dealer too."

T.J. heard the warning in Farrell's steely voice and then realized he'd been outflanked. Farrell had known he was cheating and had used it to sucker him into higher stakes! T.J. glanced nervously around the room. There was no way he could get out of this without losing his reputation. All he could do was pray for lady luck to smile on him and save his shirt!

"You wouldn't mind if we asked the Reverend Mr. Vining to deal, would you, T.J.?" It was not a question.

T.J. lowered his eyes in fury and muttered that would be just fine by him. He handed over the cards to the astonished clergyman.

"Well, I know how to shuffle and deal, of course," Peter said awkwardly, "but I don't know the game."

"It's easy, Reverend," Farrell explained with a grin. "Lowest hand wins. You deal out five cards. We bet. We get a chance to trade for two new cards if we like. And there's a bug in the deck."

Vining looked shocked.

Farrell laughed and stretched back in his chair.

"A joker, Reverend. A joker."

"Oh," mumbled Vining as he made his first attempt at shuffling. He hoped his bishop didn't get wind of this. He most sincerely hoped that.

T.J. anted, but this time Farrell could see a thin line of sweat on Walker's upper lip. T.J. wasn't talking much anymore, either. He was focusing every ounce of attention on his cards. And his money.

Farrell bet and narrowed his eyes.

He had T.J. right where he wanted him. Now he was going to move in for the kill.

It wasn't a kill. It was a slaughter.

The bets were big now. Each round of betting saw $30,000 in the pot. When it was time to show your cards the prize was running close to $100,000. Farrell took it all with cold, relentless professionalism. He'd won and lost pots that size over the years. He'd long ago learned how to look at the cash at times like this. It was just an investment to leverage your game. It was capital you risked when you calculated the odds to be leaning in your favor.

T.J. had never learned to see it that way.

When Walker saw the cash on the table his greedy little heart said "It's mine!" His hands itched to rake it in. It represented all the things he'd like to enjoy. And T.J. devoted himself to enjoying life at every chance he had. Lean, hard living was not appealing to T. J. Walker.

But that wasn't the fatal Achilles' heel that Farrell had seen in his opponent. There was another, more dangerous weakness that T.J. possessed.

T.J. couldn't stand to lose.

He absolutely could not stand it.

And that dread possibility was staring him in the face as Farrell confidently raked in the winnings of their latest hand.

T.J. wiped his face with a handkerchief and shifted uncomfortably in the chair. He barely had enough cash to stay in the game now, since the stakes were so high. He was reddening in humiliation and fury and frustration. He'd give half his possessions to be able to reach across the table and strangle Farrell. If the room weren't packed with law-abiding people, that's exactly what he'd have done!

Farrell neatly stacked the bills in their proper piles, letting T.J. sweat in his own quandary a little longer. Now he was ready to execute the final piece of his strategy against the Walkers. He could almost taste victory, and it was sweet. Almost, not quite.

The game wasn't over until the last card was played, he reminded himself.

He touched the tips of his fingers together, forming a steeple with his hands, and stared thoughtfully over them at the wary heir to the Walker fortunes. Silence had fallen over the card parlor. You could have heard a pin drop.

"Since I seem to have a tad bit more cash than you," Farrell pointed out coolly, spearing T.J. with hard, unwavering eyes, "it seems you'll need some kind of credit or IOU for us to play a last hand. Wouldn't you agree?"

T.J. gaped at Farrell in surprise.

"You mean you'd waive the standard rule . . . cash only!" T.J. exclaimed in amazement. This was his last chance to best this bastard. He couldn't believe Farrell was willing to chance it. "What would you take? An IOU?"

Farrell smiled coldly and shook his head.

"Oh, no, T.J. I didn't get where I am by being that stupid," he replied in a hardening voice. "If you were a pro, I might do it. I've left this much money on a table and gone out for dinner when I'm playing with professionals." He leaned forward and gave T.J. a contemptuous look. "And it's always there when I get back, T.J. Every last nickle and dime!" Farrell relaxed back into his chair and continued, more neutrally, "But with amateurs"—T.J. reddened in anger—"you have to be a little more careful. I've got a shoe box full of IOUs and bad checks that upstanding businessmen, ranchers, farmers, and store owners have welched on."

T.J. glared back angrily. He'd whip Farrell if it was the last thing he ever did, he swore. T. J. Walker didn't have to sit here and be talked to like this. No sirree.

"I'll tell you what, T.J. . . . I'm willing to let you write me a check if you lose." Farrell saw Samuel Walker lean forward in his chair. "How's that?"

T.J. was all ready to jump at it when his father intervened.

"This has gone far enough!" roared the old man, who'd been growing more and more livid as the game had gone on.

His son had lost most of his money and some that belonged to them both. But if he wrote a check to cover this loss, the bank couldn't cover it! Then everyone would know how deeply in trouble the bank really was.

Sam stood up and started out the back. Farrell grabbed him by the shoulder just outside the room as the people inside buzzed with opinions about the turn of events.

"Walker," Farrell said coldly, pinning the man to the wall behind him, "I feel like we've already met. Ever since I've been here I've been learning about you."

Walker angrily tried to brush Farrell's hand away.

"What do you want?" snapped the banker. He hadn't gotten where he was by beating around the bush.

Farrell shoved the man a little harder against the wall.

"I want you to leave Kate McKendrick and her family alone," Farrell said succinctly, every word packing the promise that if Walker failed to do just that, he'd have the gambler to answer to.

"I don't know what you're talking about," the banker said coldly.

Farrell twisted the lapels a little higher.

"I think you do. And I'll tell you one more thing. If anything else happens, the people in this town are going to know what's going on at that bank of yours, Walker."

The banker froze.

Farrell grinned coldly.

"Now . . . we're going back inside and you're going to tell T.J. you're proud to back him up and he's welcome to write a check to cover his losses if I win. Because if you don't, the bank examiners are going to be here before you can walk out the door, Walker. I promise you."

Walker stared into the granite determination of the younger man and knew the taste of defeat. He still might be able to straighten out the bank's problems over the course of a year, but there was nothing he could do before then. Farrell had him.

"All right," Walker said bitingly. "You seem to be holding all the cards, as they say."

"That's right, Walker," Farrell said coldly, eyes glittering with fury at the man who'd been making Kate's life hell. "I do."

Kate pulled up the mare and stared at the hard-packed snow. There were cattle tracks everywhere. And here and there she could make out cat tracks. She figured the cat must have located the herd and would now be stalking it if it was hungry enough. What bothered her was the small, bloody carcass that lay on the ground.

Kate dismounted and took a closer look.

It was a rabbit. And not too far away were horse tracks.

She frowned in concentration, trying to make sense of the confusing evidence. And then a possibility began to dawn on her. A very unpleasant possibility.

She remounted and headed the mare in the direction the horse tracks had come. Maybe she was wrong, she thought. Who'd be trying to lure a mountain lion into her ranch, anyway? she asked herself. That didn't make any sense at all!

It was the last bet of the last hand.

T.J. had drawn one card. Farrell had kept his original five.

T.J. stared at his cards and prayed they were good enough. He finally had a good hand. Ace two four seven nine. That was a nine high. He was still sweating like a pig. Everything the Walkers had built up over the years was at stake now. T.J. was desperate to hang on to it. Desperate.

T.J. wrote his last bet on a piece of paper and shoved it into the pile—$200,000. Farrell had to put all he had left in to stay in the game now. T.J. held his breath and prayed as hard as he could for lady luck to smile on him just this one last time.

Farrell looked at his own hand and looked up at T.J. T.J. hadn't had a great hand in quite a few deals now. He was due. And for the first time in his life Farrell knew how the amateurs felt when they placed a big bet.

A cold chill squeezed his heart and spread into his gut. If he matched T.J.'s bet and called, every penny of Farrell's money was on the line. If he lost, he'd be wiped out. He'd be starting from scratch again.

It had never bothered him before. When he'd won big he'd set his mother up in her own business. She ran a hotel and restaurant down in Fresno now. He'd seen to it she would be okay. She had money in the bank and was set for her retirement years when they came around.

He'd never thought much about himself.

He stared down at the $200,000 he was about to part with. If he threw in his cards, he could still help Kate out. Half that much would solve her need for capital as a rancher for the next year or so and give her a cushion for a rainy day as well.

But if he won this bet . . . he'd have both the Walkers where he wanted them for quite a while . . . and he could still help Kate financially, if she'd let him.

If she'd let him. He saw her sweet face . . . the blush that lit up her clean-scrubbed, fresh country beauty when he teased her. . . . The wide-eyed, tender look of her after they'd made love . . . the feel of her next to him in bed . . . the laughter as they'd ridden across the range together. . . .

He looked up at Amos. Mallory was the only one who knew him well enough to read the look in his eyes. Mallory saw it. Farrell was wavering. He'd lost his betting courage. He'd found something in life worth investing in, and he didn't want to lose it.

Farrell's eyes flicked back down and he calculated the odds, forcing himself to make the decision like a pro.

He shoved the rest of his money into the pot.

"I call," Farrell said evenly.

A slow grin spread across T.J.'s face. He spread his cards faceup.

"What have you got, Farrell?" he asked, leaning forward, hardly able to wait to see the answer. I've got him, at last, T.J. thought, seeing Farrell's frozen expression. I've got him!

And then, one at a time, Farrell turned up the cards.

Five. Six. Seven. Eight.

T.J. held his breath. Farrell's cards were running a little higher than his. If the next card was a ten or higher, or anything paired with what was already showing, T.J. would win.

Farrell turned up the last card.

The joker.

"I'm calling it an ace," Farrell said, still feeling a little dazed.

T.J. stared at the hand in shock, then looked up at Farrell.

"You won," he said hoarsely, pushing himself away from the table. "Beat me with the wild card . . . eight high. One card."

T.J. was mumbling incoherently and shoving his way through the crowd like a man who wasn't seeing anyone.

Amos moved forward and spoke to the senior Walker.

"I think you owe Matt a check, Mr. Walker."

Numbly, the banker wrote out the amount and stiffly made his way through the crowd and everyone began talking at once.

Farrell leaned back in the chair and stared blankly ahead of him. He'd made a big mistake the other day, he realized. He hadn't told Kate he loved her when he'd had the chance. Maybe it wasn't too late to undo the damage. He shut his eyes and prayed it wasn't. Because at last he'd found something to live for in life. And he didn't want to lose her.

Sissy trotted along behind T.J., trying to offer him sympathy. He kept brushing her off like a fly. In front of her small trailer she grabbed his hand and pleaded with him.

"It doesn't matter, hon," she said. "Come on in and lay your head on my lap. I'll make it better."

Slowly he turned to look at her. An evil hatred filled his face. He pushed her into her trailer and closed the door. Sissy began to feel afraid and nervously backed up.

"Make it better?" he snarled. "Kate could have made it better. All she had to do was sell me some land, and none of this would have happened! But I've taken care of her. She won't have any cattle by the time that cat's finished with her herd."

"T.J., what are you talking about?" Sissy whispered, alarmed at the wild look in his eyes.

He stepped forward and twisted her arm behind her back.

"Get away from me, you dumb broad," he hissed furiously.

Farrell got back to Kate's ranch as fast as he could. When Loren told him she was still tracking the cat, he went down to the barn to saddle up his own horse and go after her. That was when he found the gray wasn't quite as fit as he'd been. There was bad swelling along one leg and the horse was favoring it.

He was standing with one foot resting on the fence, watching for some sign of her, when the sheriff pulled up in his jeep. He hurried toward Farrell, looking as worried as Farrell had ever seen him.

"I just talked to Sissy Wells in the hospital, Farrell. I can't stop long. T.J. hit her and she's mad as hell. She says he's been luring that big cat into Kate's ranch by leaving fresh-killed meat for it. If the cat's taking the bait, the herd may stampede. Anything in the way will be in big trouble."

"Thanks," Farrell said shortly.

He got his rifle and ammunition as the sheriff left.

But his blood ran cold when he heard a small voice cry out.

"It's Calamity!" Jason cried. "Mom's not on her!"

Farrell ran outside and leaped over the fence.

"Tell your grandfather I'm going after her," he shouted.

The rifle was missing, he noticed, hoping that meant it was with Kate and she could protect herself from whatever had befallen her. He shoved his own into its place and vaulted onto the horse. The mare turned and hit the hard-packed snow at a full gallop.

Kate held the rifle to her shoulder and drew a bead on the cat. The big mountain lion lowered her head and laid her ears back. She was far away from Kate and trying not to alarm the cattle foraging nearby.

Kate didn't want to shoot. She might start a stampede. They were too close to the ranch for that. Not to mention the fact that she didn't relish being trampled by her own beef.

On the other hand, she wasn't about to let the cat attack either her or the cattle without a fight.

Kate had circled back, following the cat's prints until the cattle were in sight. Then she'd seen more hoof prints and dismounted to take a closer look. The cat had taken that opportunity to scream, and Calamity had bolted for home before Kate could stop her.

Fortunately, Kate had kept her rifle in her hand. It was all that was keeping the cat at bay.

A blood-curdling scream split the air and the cat launched

itself at a small heifer that had foolishly wandered too far from the herd. The cattle raised their heads as one and instantly broke into a headlong charge across the white wasteland.

Kate sighted the cat and squeezed the trigger. She no longer had anything to lose on that score, she figured. The cat twirled in midair as it leaped toward the terrified heifer. Kate just saw the cat fall in a lifeless heap before the stampeding cattle obscured it from sight.

The herd was coming straight at her.

She ran toward the drop-off just above the creek where an ancient black oak's gnarled limbs spread in skeletal silence. She hoped there might be a small chance the fear-crazed cattle would automatically split on either side of it. She'd just about reached it when she realized she wasn't going to make it. The thundering hoofs were coming too close too fast. She gave it everything she had and almost made the edge when she heard the crack of a nearby rifle.

She slid down the snowy embankment and aimed her rifle toward the herd just in time to see Farrell riding hard alongside the leaders on her mare. Calamity was lathered and looking ready to drop any minute from exhaustion. Farrell aimed his rifle and shot again. Kate saw one of the leaders fall just as he reached her. He leaped off the mare and straight onto Kate, rolling them both down the bank into the huge roots of the tree just as the cattle poured over them like the end of the world.

Kate felt his body flinch and go limp. Something had struck him. Something died inside her.

Please, God, she prayed. Don't let him die. Don't let him die.

And then the thundering began to fade as the last stragglers leaped over the two people lying just under the lip of the embankment. When she was sure no more hoofs would be jumping over them, Kate rolled Farrell's heavy, limp form off her.

Anxiously, she slipped an arm under his head and smoothed the dark lock of hair back from his forehead. Blood marked her hand. He'd been nicked by a hoof on the back of the head. The gash was bleeding freely. She sobbed and pressed her hand against it to staunch the flow.

"Matt!" she cried. "Matt!"

His eyelids flickered and gradually opened. He groaned and tried to sit.

"Don't you dare move!" she sobbed. "If you do, I'll kill you, Matt Farrell!"

He managed a weak grin and shut his eyes to stop the world from spinning so much.

"I think your cattle just about managed that," he said in a thin whisper.

Kate lowered her head as tears began streaming down her cheeks.

"Hey," he murmured, opening his eyes as he felt the first warm splash on his face, "I'm okay. I just forgot to keep my head down," he joked.

Kate just cried harder and he pulled her close to his chest.

"Katherine McKendrick," he said huskily. "You are never, I repeat *never*, to go hunting mountain lion without me again. Agreed?"

Kate clutched him and nodded yes and then realized what he had said.

"How can I promise that?" she asked in confusion. "You're leaving."

He looked up at her and swallowed. What if she hadn't meant it the way he did? What if she loved him, but not enough? He knew there was only one way to find out.

"Well, I came back to talk to you about that, as a matter of fact," he began, trying to dredge up the right words to put it to her.

Kate's eyes were big and luminous as she gazed back at him in complete mystification. His arrival had taken her totally by surprise in more ways than one. But she was so deeply happy to have him back again, she was almost without words.

"I won the poker game," he said, rather lamely.

"Congratulations," Kate murmured, misery clouding her eyes again. "You came back to tell me that?" she asked, pain threading her voice.

"No," he said softly, raising a hand to caress her soft cheek. "I came back to tell you I discovered something in the process."

He looked up at her seriously, and for once he didn't try to hide his feelings from her in any way at all. There was admiration, and affection, and concern, and longing . . . all there for her to see. And just a trace of insecurity.

Kate blinked back the last few tears and tried to take it all in.

186

"What was that?" she asked in a whisper, drowning in the love so clear in his face.

"That I love you, Kate," he murmured, his voice cracking as he recalled how close he'd just come to losing her. He pulled her close and hugged her until she thought her ribs might crack. "Damn but I love you," he said raggedly.

He loosened his hold and covered her face with kisses. They were lingering, warm, tender, passionate brands of his love for her. She melted into him and their lips fused in a soul-wrenching kiss that left them both shaking.

"I've got a lot of cash sitting around here somewhere, Kate," he said as he forced himself to finish what he wanted to say while he could still say it. "And I don't think gambling is my kind of investment anymore. I was wondering . . ."

Kate looked at him tenderly and ran her finger lightly across his lips.

"What were you wondering?" she asked him encouragingly.

"Would you consider taking me on as a partner?" he asked, holding his breath.

He'd laid himself at her mercy. Kate smiled and kissed him gently on the mouth.

"What kind of partnership did you have in mind?" she asked, a teasing gleam in her eyes.

"The kind that lasts a lifetime. . . ." he murmured huskily.

Kate snuggled against him happily.

"Does it involve any particular sleeping arrangements?" she teased, laughing.

Farrell rolled her over until he was on top and tried his best to look intimidating.

"Yes it does, damn it! Are you going to marry me? Or do I have to camp out on your ranch and make a nuisance of myself until you give in?" he threatened.

Kate looped her hands around his neck and pulled his head down to hers.

"Think you're ready to take the gamble?" she asked gently, giving him a loving smile.

He kissed her tenderly and gazed lovingly at her happy face.

"Anytime, anywhere, anyplace," he swore, sealing it with a kiss that promised forever.

Loren hobbled over the last rise with Jason scrambling along-side him. When they saw Kate and Matt lying in the snow and kissing as if there were no tomorrow, they both came to a halt.

"Does that mean Matt's staying?" Jason asked in confusion. Loren chuckled.

"I wouldn't be at all surprised, Jason."

Jason's fingers clenched over his magic stone. In a way he was very relieved to hear that. He'd been struggling all day with himself over what to give Matt as a good-bye present.

"I'm glad," Jason announced in his most grown-up voice. Loren's eyebrows ascended in adult amusement.

"Why's that?" he asked.

" 'Cause now I don't have to give Matt my magic stone that I found down there in the creek," he hurriedly explained.

Jason stretched out his hand and held it out for his grandfather to look at. There, in the middle of the small palm, lay a gold nugget the size of a robin's egg.

Loren McKendrick stared in astonishment and let out a low whistle.

"Well, I'll be!" he exclaimed. "Looks like that creek really is a source of magic!" He looked down at Kate and Matt, still in each other's loving arms and grinned. "Well, I'll be!"

Rebels and outcasts, they fled halfway across the earth to settle the harsh Australian wastelands. Decades later—ennobled by love and strengthened by tragedy—they had transformed a wilderness into fertile land. And themselves into

The Australians

WILLIAM STUART LONG

THE EXILES, #1	12374-7-12	$3.95
THE SETTLERS, #2	17929-7-45	$3.95
THE TRAITORS, #3	18131-3-21	$3.95
THE EXPLORERS, #4	12391-7-29	$3.95
THE ADVENTURERS, #5	10330-4-40	$3.95
THE COLONISTS, #6	11342-3-21	$3.95

All-new
Candlelight Newsletter

**An exceptional,
free offer awaits readers
of Dell's incomparable Candlelight Ecstasy and Supreme Romances.**

Subscribe to our all-new CANDLELIGHT NEWSLETTER and you will receive—at absolutely no cost to you—exciting, exclusive information about today's finest romance novels and novelists. You'll be part of a select group to receive sneak previews of upcoming Candlelight Romances, well in advance of publication.

You'll also go behind the scenes to "meet" our Ecstasy and Supreme authors, learning firsthand where they get their ideas and how they made it to the top. News of author appearances and events will be detailed, as well. And contributions from the Candlelight editor will give you the inside scoop on how she makes her decisions about what to publish—and how *you* can try your hand at writing an Ecstasy or Supreme.

You'll find all this and more in Dell's CANDLELIGHT NEWSLETTER. And best of all, *it costs you nothing.* That's right! It's Dell's way of thanking our loyal Candlelight readers and of adding another dimension to your reading enjoyment.

Just fill out the coupon below, return it to us, and look forward to receiving the first of many CANDLELIGHT NEWS-LETTERS—overflowing with the kind of excitement that only enhances our romances!

EUCLID PUBLIC LIBRARY